ALL
your
LIES

AMARIE COLLINS

To the ones who want a sweet man with a deliciously dark and gritty edge.

Content Information

Dear reader,

This book contains dark themes that may be triggering.

PTSD, Anxiety, Paranoia, Car Accident, Kidnapping, Food Aversions, Stalking, Abusive and Neglectful Parents, Weapon and Drug Trafficking, Drug Use, Alcohol Consumption, Restaurant Fire, Sick Parent, Mentions of Sex Trafficking, Torture and Body Mutilation, Murder and Death, Home Invasion and Destruction of Property, Severe bodily harm by gunfire, Suicidal Ideation, Dubious Consent, Organized Crime.

Playlist

"Electric Love" – Borns

"Mind (feat. Kai)" – Jack U, Skrillex, & Diplo

"Make Me Fade" – K. Flay

"Bloodstream"– Stateless

"Just want you to feel something" – Artemas

"Closer"– Nine Inch Nails

"Planez"– Jeremih

"Feel so close" – Calvin Harris

"Glad you came" – the wanted

"Heaven"– Julia Michaels

"If You Wanna" – Kiyashqo

"Ocean Eyes" – Billie Eilish

"I Wanna Be Yours" – Arctic Monkeys

"Sweater weather" – The Neighbourhood

"Stay" – Ari Abdul

"Love Is Complicated (The Angels Sing)" – Labrinth

"Sure Thing" – Miguel

"Eyes don't lie" – Isabel LaRosa

"Fucked Up Kinda Dream" – Artemas
"Home" –Good Neighbours
"Gasoline & Flowers" – Dutch Melrose
"Mess of me, sexually" – Artemas
"Power Trip"– J. Cole
"LET THEWORLD BURN" – Chris Grey
"Sweet" –Cigarettes After Sex

One

Alexa

S tartled by the pulsing lights from the white car behind me, I swiftly change lanes to grant them passage. One of my biggest pet peeves is inconsiderate drivers who believe they have exclusive rights to the road or, even worse, individuals who neglect to use their blinkers. I wait for them to get beside me just so I can see their stupid, impatient face, but they get into the right lane behind me again.

My spine shivers with an icy sensation, yet I resist the temptation to jump to conclusions of kidnapping, assault, or assassination.

Perhaps it's a generous soul trying to inform me about a flat tire or a malfunctioning blinker. But wouldn't my car notify me if something was wrong? I could kick myself for not paying closer attention when Dad explained the ins and outs of basic car maintenance.

With each turn I take, my stomach churns with unease as I watch the car behind mirror my path and maintain a steady speed behind me. I speed up; they speed up. I turn; they turn.

Desperate to end this gut-wrenching feeling, I make a hard right and slingshot my car between two office buildings. The echo of my engine reverberates off the walls, signaling my location, but I don't dare turn my car off in case I have to make a speedy getaway.

Just as my tires screech to a halt, I anxiously reach for the handle of the center console. As I rip the small compartment door open, I can hear the clatter of objects inside before my fingertips finally graze the metal of my gun. It would be faster to use my eyes, but I can't risk averting my gaze from my rearview mirror.

Just as I feel the cold metal of the barrel in my palm, the car that's been tailing me comes to a sudden stop behind me.

I can't believe this is happening to me again.

With tremors in my right hand, I fight to keep my gun steady. The click of the safety rings through my ears as I clumsily disengage it, sending a rush of adrenaline through my veins. I conceal the gun at my right side just as someone comes to my window and knocks twice.

My heart pounds in my ears, drowning out all other sounds as I gaze over at... Brad?

With a loud clank, my gun slips free from my hand and lands on the floorboard as I roll down my car window.

"Are you okay?" he asks with a furrowed brow as he leans his head closer to my open window.

"Why are you following me?"

"You left your coat at work. I thought you might need it."

He raises his arm in my line of sight so I can see my black coat I always keep in the office for chilly days draped over his forearm.

I feel foolish.

"Right, sorry." I grab my jacket from him and pull it through my window. "Thanks."

"Of course. Are you sure you're okay? You look scared."

"I'm fine," I say, forcing a smile. *Never show vulnerability, Alexandria.* My dad's words echo through my mind. "I'll see you Monday. Have a good weekend."

Before he can utter another word, I roll my window up. From here on out, he'll probably think I'm crazy. I guess that's a win. Now he won't ask me to go out with him and our coworkers.

He stares at me for a beat longer before heading back to his car. As he slowly drives by, I can sense him gazing over at me, but I keep my eyes trained on my steering wheel and my trembling hands in my lap.

The heightened sense of adrenaline no longer runs through my veins. Instead, crippling anxiety and tension consume me.

I grab the rib-knit hem of my long-sleeved black cashmere sweater and rip it over my head while praying the feeling of suffocation fades. Each breath I take is a chaotic dance of uneven, choppy inhales and exhales as if I'm being strangled.

Dr. Schults's instructions echo in my mind at moments like this, guiding me through my impending panic. My head whips around, scanning the surroundings as I double-check that I'm alone and my doors are locked. I lower my head onto the black leather steering wheel before shutting my eyes as I take deliberate, deep breaths. In the depths of my mind, a calming aqua-blue orb emits a soft, gentle glow, casting a serene ambiance throughout the dark room of my mind. As the orb projects its light, the black walls come alive with a dazzling, vivid display of swirling colors and ever-changing shapes.

As I unwind, I feel the tension in my jaw release, followed by a soothing sensation in my neck, shoulders, and eventually, my whole body. Three-second inhale, three-second exhale. Three-second inhale, three-second exhale.

You are safe. You are alive. You are strong.

The last one always leaves a bitter taste in my mouth.

Even after thirty minutes of visualization and diaphragmatic breathing, it still can't keep me from the truth of my inadequacies.

How am I supposed to become a Mafia boss? How am I supposed to lead others? I'm just as useless as I was before.

The scared girl turned into the scared woman.

Two

Alexa

15 YEARS OLD

"Again, Alexandria," Dad huffs.

"I got it, Dad. I'm tired, and I just want to shower and relax."

We've sparred for hours. I have sweat dripping from my elbows, my limbs are shaking, and I can already tell I'm going to be sore as hell for the rest of the month if we keep going.

"You don't have it. You're getting sloppy with your movements. We don't have the luxury of weakness. I want you strong, and I want to be sure you can take care of yourself."

"Dad," I say with a small smile. He's always so worried about me. "I'll be fine. You've trained me since I took my first steps. You have nothing to worry about. Besides, Marco will be by my side."

My dad scowls at the mention of Marco, my future husband, even though he's the one who made the agreement with Marco's father years ago. I understand his reservations. Marco has had a hard time dealing with things.

"That isn't good enough. There will be times when you're alone." He shakes his head.

"But—"

"Again," Dad says as he gets back into his stance and hits his gloved hands together.

"I said I'll be fine!" I shout at him and immediately regret it when he winces.

He's always handled me gently and with great care, even during my combat training, but he's been on edge. Ever since Gage, Marco, and my best friend, Rosie's, brother went to prison, my dad's concern for my safety has reached new heights. He won't tell me why when I ask, but I'm aware things have changed within the families.

The thought of Gage brings a knot to my throat and burning behind my eyes. You'd think after him being gone for two hundred and seventy-three days, I'd be past the crying stage or counting the days, but I'm not. It also doesn't help that he refuses to acknowledge me or my letters. It fucking hurts. He's supposed to be my safe place, my rock.

"I'm sorry, Alexandria," Dad says as he looks down at the red-and-black checkerboard mat.

"No, I'm sorry. I shouldn't have yelled at you. I'm just tired from swim practice."

"I understand. We can stop for the day."

"Thank you!" I wrap my arms around him. My dad is one of a kind, and I doubt there will ever be someone who treats me as he does.

Gage's face comes to mind, and I shake my head to dislodge the thought. I can't break down right now, not in front of my dad.

I need to be strong.

Even though my dad is being tough on me today, he's proud of me and believes I'm capable of taking his place as Capo.

I can't let him down.

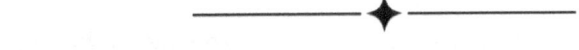

ONE WEEK LATER

"Don't worry, Ro. It's okay," I say while waving at my parents, who are getting into their black Mercedes across the school parking lot.

"I'm just sorry I couldn't be there," Rosie says with a hint of guilt.

"Your art exhibit is a big deal. I always have swim meets. Plus, my mom and dad came this time. It's no biggie."

"Still, this was finals. I know how important it was to you. I think I already know the answer, but I have to ask. Did Marco come?"

"Has he ever?" I say with a defeated huff.

"No." She sighs. "I just thought...now that Gage is gone, he'd step up. For you and for me."

A tear leaks out of my eye and I don't even bother brushing it away. It's not like anyone will see me shed a few tears for Gage in the dark, deserted parking lot. I let it fall from my cheek with a few more in tow before hopping into my car and driving out of the school.

"Marco is going through a lot," I say, defending him for the millionth time. Maybe if I continue to say it, I'll start to believe it myself.

Marco has never been very thoughtful or even sweet toward me, but he's going to be my husband. We have to make it work. Mom *says sometimes it takes men longer to pull their head out of their ass. He must be one of those guys.*

I stop at a light and squint into my rearview mirror against the headlights of the truck behind me. The jerk must not realize their brights are on. It's as if someone is pointing a floodlight into the back of my car.

"Are you there?" Rosie asks as I continue to gaze at the idiot behind me.

"Yeah, I'll be over soon. Are you still down for a movie marathon? I can get Thai," I say, knowing it's her favorite.

"I'm so down. My father brought Manuel over again. I hope Mama can talk him out of this stupid arranged marriage. I can't do it, Lex. I'll die before letting it happen."

Alarm bells ring in my ears as I hear the desperation in her voice. "Hey, don't say that. It'll be okay. We'll figure something out, I promise."

"Okay," Rosie whispers.

"I'll see you soon, and we'll brainstorm over food."

"Deal. See you soon."

The light turns green as soon as I hang up. The asshole behind me blares his horn as if I've let the light stay green for more than a mere two seconds.

"Okay, geez." I step on the gas and floor it through the intersection, then make the first right, leaving the black truck in my dust.

I grab my phone and look up The Thai House. Hopefully they haven't closed yet. It's kind of late, but from the way Rosie sounded on the phone, she needs her favorite comfort food.

I couldn't imagine being betrothed to Manuel. He's a real psychopath and would never treat her the way she deserves. I guess I should count my lucky stars that Marco isn't that bad.

My finger hovers over The Thai House call button when I'm thrust into my steering wheel with a bang, sending my phone flying and a pain in my chest from hitting the steering wheel. I glare into my rearview mirror at the truck from before.

Did it just hit me?

My eyes widen, and I gasp when its headlights come too close to my car and ram it again.

"A-Alexa," I gasp as I yell at my phone. It's never been so hard to say my own name.

"Alexa," I repeat. "Call Dad!"

The seconds for my phone to understand my words are excruciating. "Calling... Dad," the phone app assistant says.

"Alexandria," Dad says over my car speaker.

"Dad," I whimper like it's a prayer.

"Alexandria?"

"Someone's following me. They—they..."

"Focus, Alexandria," he says in a stern voice. "Where are you?"

"I-I don't know," I say frantically as I continue to drive down dark roads far too fast.

"Check her location," Dad yells to someone.

I scream as the truck hits the back of my car again.

"Hurry, Dad. Please," I sob.

"Do you have your gun?"

"Yes, but I can't—"

"You can. Get it!" he barks out.

Just as I'm reaching over, a white van pulls in front of me and slams on its brakes. I swerve hard to the left to get out of the way, making my passenger side scrape along the side of their car.

"Someone stopped in front of me."

9

"Fuck," Dad mutters. "Take the next left-hand turn. Then gun it, Alexandria."

"Okay," I say just as I turn, then look behind me. There are no lights in my rearview anymore. "They're gone."

"Do you have your gun?"

"No. I haven't—"

"Get it now!"

I stretch my body across the car with a huff and pull open the passenger glovebox. I take my eyes off the road to reach in and retrieve the gun when my car gets hit again.

A scream rips through my throat as my car spins out of control before coming to a stop against something hard.

Dots blur my vision as I try to scan my surroundings. I'm so dizzy, and my head feels like it got hit with a sledgehammer. I rub my fingers against my temple and pull it back when I feel something wet. Something dark and sticky is on my fingers. I bring my fingers closer to my face to inspect it when the glass of my window gets shattered, and I'm wrenched out by my hair.

I let out another piercing scream as glass shards slice through my side on the way out. The hand in my hair doesn't leave as I'm dragged across the unforgiving ground. I desperately try to break free with my nails embedded in the hand of my attacker that's attached to my strands of hair while my other hand tries to grip the dirt tightly. I feel the sharp sting as my nails dig into the earth and snap as I try to prevent my attacker from dragging me any farther.

It's futile.

He's bigger and stronger.

The sound of tires screeching and lights getting closer fills me with worry about being run over, but it could be the lesser evil compared to the attacker's intentions. Inches away from us, the car comes to a halt, and the door swings open with a loud creak.

The air grows heavy as I fix my eyes on my dad. His hand is steady as he aims the barrel of the gun above me. A mixture of hope and dread fills me.

The man releases my hair, but it's too late.

An eerie stillness replaces the piercing sound of the gunshot, with only a faint thud breaking the silence behind me.

My eyes meet my dad's as he tucks the gun away in its holster beneath his jacket and approaches me with a determined stride.

His eyes usually sparkle with love, but what I see now is worry and rage.

I cast my eyes to the ground, unable to bear the intensity.

I choked.

The heir to his empire choked.

I let myself down. But worse, I let him down.

"The coordinates I sent require cleanup. Alexandria's first."

My head snaps up to observe my dad and his blatant lie as he speaks into his phone.

I shake my head at him, but he doesn't acknowledge me.

Rule 1: "To become an heir and rightfully rule, one must take the life of another before their eighteenth birthday."

Three

Alexa

A large gust of wind blows in my face, causing me to bring in a startled gasp as my eyes spring open.

Jenna's face is inches from mine. Her gray-blue eyes sparkle with mischief.

"Jesus, you scared the shit out of me."

A Cheshire cat smile tugs at her lips. "I'm glad you're awake. We should hit the spa."

"It's Friday." I grumble.

"Thank you, Captain Obvious. If you get ready now, we can beat all the geriatric cougars and get one of the hot massage therapists."

"Pass. I have to work," I say as I stretch and get out of bed.

"Stop being so sensible. It's not even your actual job, Mafia Madame."

"Ugh. It's called a capo, and I should've never told you."

"Umm, yes, you should have. My best friend is going to be a Mafia boss. How badass."

"There's absolutely nothing badass about me," I say as I think about my freak-out yesterday. To quiet my restless mind and ensure a peaceful night's sleep, I had to rely on a sleeping pill once I got home. That's not badass. It's pitiful.

"You just haven't come into your powers yet, is all."

"I never knew murder and racketeering were powers."

"On the contrary, it takes a lot of finesse." Jenna's stone-cold, serious face makes me smile. She strikes a balance between being lighthearted and an eccentric, silly psycho.

"Those true crime documentaries you love so much are going to rot your brain."

She shrugs. "Knowledge is power."

"You know, if you were smart, you'd run in the other direction. Why don't you?"

"Easy," Jenna says as she winds her long platinum-blond hair into a chaotic, messy bun. "I have no self-preservation."

"Obviously." I smile.

Her face turns serious as she looks me dead in the eyes. "You will be a phenomenal leader, though."

"How do you have so much faith in me?"

"Easy. I don't become friends with lames. Now, get up. I want to be rubbed out within an inch of my life."

"Gross," I say, scrunching my nose. "Like I said, I have to work. I swear you're like Ten Second Tom."

"Who the hell's that?"

"Just a character in a movie," I say as I turn off my alarm, which still won't go off for another hour, thanks to Jenna's early wake-up call. "You know, you should watch more movies. You're missing out."

"So, this Ten Second Tom, is he gorgeous with an amazing personality and undeniable humor?"

"He suffers from short-term memory loss, where he forgets what happens after ten seconds."

"Fucking rude." Jenna pauses while looking confused. "What were you saying?"

"You—"

"Kidding. So that's the premise of the story? What a bore."

"No, it's about a woman who loses her memory after an accident and can't remember anything the day before. This guy meets her and falls hard, only to find out she can't remember him the next day. He spends the movie trying to get her to remember him."

"I'm not even the main character?" She frowns.

"Not this time." I laugh. "It's a good movie, though."

"Does she ever remember him?" she asks. Something close to hope enters her eyes but is gone in a matter of seconds.

"Yes and no. He makes a tape for her to watch every morning to remember who he is. He never stops trying."

"That sounds exhausting."

"It's always worth it for the right person."

"Geez, you're sappy this morning. Don't touch me. I don't want to catch it." Jenna makes a cross with her fingers as if to ward me off. I roll my eyes at her silliness.

"You'll fall in love one day and totally eat your words. I can't wait."

"Fat fucking chance. Okay, back to the point. We're going out tonight."

"I'd rather stay in. Maybe—"

"No. You're coming. Be ready by eight. They stop letting people in at nine."

"Why would they do that?"

"Fuck if I know. Just be ready." Jenna swats my ass and saunters past me.

As I sit down for my lunch break, I can't help but marvel at how quickly the day is passing. The thought of being free from this place and having two days off in the sunshine and not in a cubicle is making me restless.

My mom's influence and connections helped me land a job at a local non-profit even though I lacked experience and formal qualifications. She's a generous supporter of this specific charity that helps children in need, and when my mom reached out to them, they couldn't refuse.

I also didn't refuse when my mom brought up the idea of me working here. It felt like a way to atone for my future transgressions. Sins I'm still grappling with. Helping people in need now only to snuff out the lives of others later.

It's kind of fucked up for me to believe working here will somehow cleanse my soon-to-be bloody hands.

It won't.

Nothing will.

The path to becoming the head of the Rossi Family, following my father, is fraught with opposition and difficult battles, each one testing my resolve and resilience. Many in the other families are vehemently against a woman leading. The consensus is my cousin Vinny, a powerful and established made man, deserves the inheritance. I need to prove to everyone, including myself, that I have what it takes as one of the first females to lead. The enormity of the task ahead is daunting, and I dread it.

This is part of the reason I'm here at the job that Jenna considers my "fake job." I want to relish in the simple pleasures of a normal nine-to-five before being thrust into life-and-death situations. Experiencing normalcy unrestricted and unburdened is my goal.

The insistent buzzing of my phone jolts me from my reverie, so I quickly fish it out of my handbag.

Jenna

> Just had the most mind-blowing massage.

Alexa

> TMI

Jenna

> Prude. And don't even think about backing out tonight. If you do, I'll find you.

Well yeah, she'll find me. She's my next-door neighbor, so I couldn't hide from her, even if I wanted to.

I sense someone staring at me, and as I glance up from my phone, Brad, from yesterday, fills my vision. I smile at him before peering down at my phone as it vibrates with another message.

Jenna

> I also took the liberty of purchasing you a dress. It's sure to get you laid.

Alexa

> You being so worried about my sex life is kind of weird.

Jenna

> I'm just a concerned friend.

I snort but stop when I hear a throat clear and raise my eyes. Brad is still staring at me while leaning against the counter. In contrast to everyone else's relaxed attire for business casual Friday, his dark blue suit seems out of place in the office.

"Good afternoon, Mr. Brown," I say before taking a bite of my forgotten lunch.

"Alexa. Please, call me Brad."

He's told me this countless times, but I use his last name to create a barrier between us. A first-name basis will make him believe we're friends. He's nice, but doesn't get the hint I'm not interested.

I give a slight nod while aimlessly pushing my food around on the plate.

"I wanted to talk about yesterday—"

"There's no need," I say, not wanting to rehash my panic attack.

"I just didn't want you to think I was stalking you or anything."

With a shake of my head, I glance upward at him. "I don't."

"That's good. A few of us are going out for drinks. You should come with us this time. I can pick you up at your place around seven."

"I have plans already, but thank you for the invite," I say with a slight smile.

Not once have I gone out with anyone from work. Most keep their distance because they are aware of my identity and my family's infamous reputation. Though Brad seems to be immune since he has asked multiple times, like a broken record. I don't have a problem with him, but he's always given me a weird vibe.

Maybe he's just socially awkward? I can't fault the guy for that, as I too am socially awkward.

However, I always go with my gut. Trusting outsiders is bad for business.

"Okay. Some other time," he murmurs before making a quick exit from the lunchroom.

"Sure," I say to the empty room.

My phone rings at five o'clock on the dot. Jenna can be needy as hell sometimes. I roll my eyes as I answer the phone.

"I barely walked out of work, and I already said I'm going—"

"Going where, Alexandria?"

"Oh, Dad. Hi," I say as I start my car.

"And where's my princess going?"

"Uh, dinner," I blurt.

"I'd be proud of how well a lie rolls off your tongue if it wasn't directed at me."

I grimace. He's always been a human lie detector.

"Sorry, Jenna and I are going out to a club."

"I will arrange—"

"No, Dad. I don't want any bodyguards. They always hover, and I end up getting a bunch of weird looks from people."

The mere thought of people staring at me, especially with my dad's overdressed guards standing beside me like silent sentries, fills me with crippling dread. I'll be surrounded by watchful eyes, and any movement toward me will be met with an instant aggressive response. I don't want anyone getting hurt because of me.

It was a miracle I'm able to live by myself now. It took a combination of convincing, prayers, and almost a sacrifice to make it happen.

"Fine," Dad says, resigned. "Bring a gun."

"Only if it matches my dress," I joke. Something my old self would have done. He doesn't know how badly the incident six years ago fucked me up, and he never will.

Now, I never leave home without a gun or, at the very least, a knife on me, just in case. I know I should have a guard with me. It's unwise not to, particularly for someone in my situation, but I sensed that if I did, I'd always be plagued by self-doubt. I'm usually able to tamp down the sense of worthlessness until it's a mere whisper in the back of my mind, but then something like yesterday happens, and I'm thrust back into the high waters with a brick on my chest and no salvation of shore in sight.

"Alexandria—"

"I miss you and Mom," I say to throw him off. I don't want to talk guards, my future capo title, or my failed arranged marriage.

"We miss you too. Only a little longer and I'll have you back where you belong."

My mood tanks at the thought of coming home. "I know."

"I meant to ask," Dad sighs before dropping his voice. "It seems Rosalinda went missing. Do you know anything about that?"

Silence is my only answer.

Dad lets out another resigned sigh. "Is she safe?"

One thing I admire about my dad is his constant, unwavering support and ability to empathize with Rosie's situation. He vowed he would never coerce me into an arranged marriage, unlike the situation Rosie is facing, where her consent is not considered. He gave me the option to refuse when Marco was first brought up. It isn't standard practice, but I appreciated his consideration.

"I-I don't know. I haven't heard from her yet."

She was supposed to call me when she got to California. It was supposed to take around fifty-two hours, and she left two days ago, so she should call me soon.

"She's made quite the mess. They're ripping the city apart looking for her," my dad says as I hear muffled voices on his line. "I have a meeting I need to get to. I just wanted to call and see how my princess was doing. Be safe, Alexandria."

"I will. I love you."

"Ti Amo." I hear a click on his side of the phone.

I continue to drive with thoughts of my own future on my mind. My arranged marriage with Marco is over. Where does that leave me? I always thought he would be by my side to help in the categories I would fail in.

Now, I'm all by myself. But I'd rather be alone than with a cheater.

Four

Alexa

As I walk through my door, the thought of canceling my plans with Jenna crosses my mind as I sink deeper into exhaustion. The aftermath of yesterday's episode, combined with the late-night sleeping pill and early wake up, left me in a zombie-like state all day. Dinner in a candlelit bath with a book in hand sounds far more pleasurable than going to a club, but I suspect Jenna wouldn't approve. Since bulldozing her way into my life months ago, she's pulled me out of the house as much as possible. She's the social butterfly to my antisocial moth.

Stepping into my kitchen, I open my stainless-steel refrigerator and grab the neck of the half-full bottle of Moscato. I forgo the glass and drink it straight from the source. With its notes of peach and grapefruit, the slightly fizzy wine brings back memories of summers in Turin, Italy with my mom's side of the family. The last time we visited, we took Rosie, and I may have convinced her to join me in indulging in an entire bottle of sweet wine, just like this one, from the underground wine cellar. We

21

were so intoxicated that we dozed off amid the flowers, only to be abruptly awoken by the sprinklers dousing us the following morning. Despite the awful hangover, the memory never fails to bring a smile to my face.

I dial her burner cell, but it goes straight to voicemail again. I never liked the idea of her running by herself. It's dangerous, but I understand her need to carve her own path and find her happiness. I'm still in the process of finding mine.

I turn on my favorite hip-hop station and begin getting ready for tonight. Though I want to stay in, I realize nights like these will be a distant memory soon, and I should take advantage of the time I have.

Ready by seven fifty, I head over to Jenna's, not giving her the opportunity to search for me.

I step out onto my porch and my ankle twists on the uneven ground. A low growl escapes my lips as I curse under my breath. I swear I'm so damn clumsy sometimes.

I glance down at my front porch, and my eyes meet a half-smashed red rose. Its vibrant color contrasts against the gray concrete with its silk petals detached and scattered. I bend to retrieve it, then survey the deserted residential street.

I've sworn off all men until further notice, so this is a little weird.

Maybe they meant to put this on Jenna's porch? With a flick of my wrist, I send the crushed rose flying into the manicured bush while its petals scatter in the breeze. Then I walk next door to Jenna's.

"Knock, knock," I say through the screen door.

"It's open," she yells from the back.

I shake my head at how carefree she is. She doesn't lock her door. It's chaos in her apartment, clothes and shoes abandoned in a haphazard mess, the remnants of last night's dinner still on the counter, and a single fake eyelash clinging to her entry mirror by a thread. But she's as happy as can be.

"Damn, look at you. I knew that dress would be perfect," she says with a mischievous smile and eyebrows wagging.

I run my hand along the tight red leather corset of the midi dress. "It's so damn tight. Do you know how hard it was to get this thing on by myself? I contemplated rubbing myself down with olive oil at one point. I'll be lucky not to shred it to pieces when I take it off later."

"The red leather looks amazing with your porcelain skin and dark hair. Besides, maybe you'll find someone to take it off for you."

I scrunch my nose. "I'll pass. Are you almost ready, crazy?"

"Hell yes!"

When we arrive at our destination, a wave of confusion washes over me. My gaze sweeps across the area, revealing only crumbling, deserted industrial buildings.

I turn to Jenna and raise an eyebrow.

"Oh, where's your sense of adventure? No judging until we get inside." She pats my leg, knowing exactly what I'm thinking.

"I've heard that before. If I die, I'm coming back to haunt your ass! And where's inside? It looks empty to me," I say as my eyes scan our surroundings. Nothing good ever happens in places like this after dark.

"Looks can be deceiving. Let's go."

Jenna hops out of the car, leaving me to watch her adjust herself. She looks completely flawless, as usual. Her light blue mini dress perfectly complements her eyes, while her heels add at least half a foot to her height, giving her legs for days. It won't take over twenty minutes for her to have a guy under her spell.

I scramble out of the car far less gracefully and catch up to her. She links her arm with mine with a smile. "Ready?"

"Not even a little."

As we round the corner of the building, the soft glow of a lone yellow light catches our attention above a door. Very ominous and serial killer, if you ask me.

We stand in front of the imposing metal door, and Jenna raps on it three times. A camera positioned in the top right corner with a red blinking light captures our every action. Accompanied by a piercing screech, a small peephole materialized in the middle of the metal door, causing me to recoil. It's quite unsettling. The scene suggests a horror movie featuring someone's torture in a dungeon, with their tormentor checking on their suffering via a tiny hole.

A lone pair of eyes silently watches us, and we end up in this uncomfortable, weird stare off.

I nudge Jenna with my elbow to get her attention. This was her plan, after all.

"Oh shit. Sorry, Obsidian," she blurts.

My wide eyes travel to her, and all I can think is she's lost her fucking mind. "Obsidian?" I hiss.

In a split second, the miniature door slams shut and the enormous door creaks open.

As we walk through, we eye a massive figure. He's tall and wide and has more facial tattoos than I've ever seen.

"Spread your arms and legs."

"Excuse me?" I arch my brow.

He waves a handheld metal detector in his right hand.

Right.

I spread my arms and legs as the bouncer approaches. He begins at my face, tracing a path down my body until a *beep beep* on my right thigh forces me to shut my eyes in resignation. I halter my switchblade there so often I rarely notice it.

"Oops," I say with a nervous smile as I lean down and retrieve it, then hand it to his meaty outstretched mitt of a hand also covered in tattoos.

While the weight of the blade is barely noticeable when it's on, when it's off, it leaves behind a lingering emptiness, like a phantom limb. I attempt to mask it, but my nerves surge uncontrollably. I don't like feeling defenseless.

With curiosity, he gazes down at the switchblade, his fingers deftly pressing the button to retract the long stainless-steel blade. When he looks back at me, his brow is raised in question. Most women carry pepper spray. I probably look like a psychopath.

"Can never be too careful these days, am I right?" I ask with an awkward laugh.

His expression turns stoic as he ignores me and pockets my blade, much to my dismay. Then he turns to Jenna without uttering a word.

She gets into position, and the beeper goes off at her crotch. Her smile is mischievous as she looks at the behemoth of a man with a twinkle in her eye. I hold my breath as I sense the atmosphere shift.

"Just a bomb-ass pussy and a few piercings. You're more than welcome to check."

I almost choke as the words leave her mouth. She's out of her mind.

Stepping back, the man's arm swings toward the next door, signaling his intention to have us out of his sight.

Jenna sends him a wink before stepping next to me. "Maybe later, sexy."

"You're absolutely insane," I whisper-hiss, making her throw her head back and laugh. Yep, she's certifiable.

We proceed down the dimly lit hall. The darkness engulfs us like a cave.

My brain finally catches up, and I realize the question I was trying to ask earlier. I interrupt her mid-stride, causing her to come to a sudden halt.

"How'd you know a secret password to a place you've never been? And 'Obsidian'? What kind of open sesame password is that?"

"My coworker told me about this place. She came with some guy. It's a secret society kind of place," she whispers.

"Your coworker? The one who's an escort?"

"She's a stripper." She shrugs. "Well, and an escort."

"Are you out of your mind? Is this place even legal?" I try to keep my voice low, but each question becomes a strained whisper-shout, and my voice rises an octave at the end.

"Yes, this place is legal-ish."

"Legal-ish? That isn't even a word!"

She snorts. "First of all, Mrs. Morality Police, your family is the Mafia; you are the Mafia. A little sex club is the smallest of sins you will amass."

"I'm more worried about getting caught and having to look my dad in the eyes."

"If it gets raided, we run. No biggie. Though, from what I've heard, it's exclusive to many higher-ups. Billionaires, CEO's, senators. I doubt they'd want it to close its doors. It's like the ultimate playground for people who like to act prim and proper in public and then let their real selves come out to play."

"That doesn't make me feel any better."

"Leave your moral compass at the door and free your mind. You'll be fine for one night," she says as she pulls me forward.

"Mm-hmm, famous last words," I say to myself.

I need a drink. Or ten.

As we approach another door, its black leather upholstery stands out strangely amid the surrounding concrete walls. Jenna twists the knob, and I narrow my eyes as the brilliant white light pours out of the room. What kind of mind fuckery is this? Both the walls and the marble floors are a pure stark white. As we enter what seems to be a lobby, a woman in a tight blond bun and dressed in a black pantsuit rises from her desk.

"Welcome to Obsidian. May I scan your identification?"

I pull my ID out of the back of my phone case, opting to be as hands-free tonight as possible.

"Shit," Jenna mutters as she searches for her ID in her messy sequin clutch with no success. "Here, hold this," she instructs, and into my palm goes a smooth metal flashlight, a slightly tacky pink lip gloss tube, two red pens, three small connected paperclips, a blue sucker, a fork, a tarot card with the word death across it, and a surprisingly weighty miniature Super Woman figurine.

I raise an eyebrow at her array of weird items in my hands as she continues to rummage through her bag. "No stapler or rolling pin?" I deadpan.

"That's in my other...ah!" she exclaims as she reaches into the bodice of her dress and rips her ID out with a smile before handing it to the woman behind the desk.

"Here," I say, thrusting all of her odds and ends back into her clutch. "What's up with the figurine?"

"It's good luck."

I raise a brow. "And the tarot card?"

"Also good luck," she says with a wink.

"Welcome, Ms. Rossi and Ms. Jacobs. It seems this is your first time here, so I will have you fill these out." She passes us a thick stack of papers and a couple pens.

The NDA and waiver on the very top catch my attention, causing my eyes to widen.

Where the hell am I and why would I need that?

I reach down and pinch Jenna's leg.

"Ouch," she hisses.

I eye the woman typing on her keyboard before looking at Jenna. "An NDA?" I whisper. Jenna just smirks as she signs her life away without reading a thing.

"I can assure you it's for the benefit of every member. We take our privacy here extremely seriously," the woman says without looking up from her screen. I give her a tight smile and redirect my gaze to the rules.

I scan through three pages of club policies and guidelines.

There are strict rules on refusal; no means no, which I believe is a given, but I guess you can never be too sure.

Only one alcoholic drink is allowed for consumption by members in any attraction for the night, excluding the bar and front club area.

Attraction? Like theme park attractions?

All scenes must be agreed upon by all partners prior to beginning.

Scenes? What the hell are those?

Failure to comply with the aforementioned rules will lead to termination of membership and prosecution.

Despite reading through everything quickly, I can't help but pause at certain parts that leave me mentally scratching my head in bewilderment. Safe words? Fetishes? Dom/sub? A part of me yearns to ask questions, but the other part is crippled by a paralyzing sense of embarrassment. Yes, I've read about these things countless times, but the reality of it hits differently when you're a mere door away from being entombed by debauchery. I have no experience. It would be like taking calculus when you can't pass basic math. I'm out of my depth. Therefore, I have no intention of going anywhere besides the bar or dance floor.

The words on the page blur as I scanned the document, but when I finally reach the membership fee, my jaw drops, and my eyes widened in disbelief.

I lean in toward Jenna's ear. "Twenty-five grand for the introductory membership fee!? Are you fucking insane?"

"Definitely." Jenna smiles.

"I can't afford this."

Jenna scoffs. "You're worth millions. I don't understand why you act so weird about money all the time."

"It's called being frugal. It allows you to keep having money."

"And boring, you can't forget that. You only have one life to live, Lex. Live it."

"I'm trying to, but this is crazy," I say.

"Chill, I'm going to pay for it."

"You suddenly have another job besides bartending I don't know about?"

"No, but I have this pretty cool plastic thing with a black strip on the back."

She can't be serious. I regard her as if she's lost her mind for the millionth time tonight. "No way are you using your credit card on this."

"So you want to use yours, then?" she asks with a cheeky grin.

"Absolutely not. My parents get my statements. I'd be mortified."

"Then it's settled. I'll pay for the first month. If you don't like it, cancel the membership. See, easy peasy. Now sign the damn thing and stop stalling. I want to see what all the fuss is about," she pleads as she points at all the places I need to sign.

"I'm paying you back when we get home. This is too much." I shake my head, then sign the remaining lines.

"Perfect," the woman says while gazing through the stack of papers to make sure we signed all the fields, then gazes up at us. "Ms. Rossi, may I see your right wrist?"

"Is the blood sacrifice next?" I mutter.

The woman laughs. "You're funny. I like you already."

"Thanks?" I say, quirking an eyebrow.

She places a one-inch black band with a small screen around both of our right wrists.

"This bracelet will allow you to move throughout the different rooms and attractions. You place it on the screen like this, and it will read your band. If access is granted, the bracelet's screen will light up green and the door will unlock. If you are not permitted, it will remain black. This works much like a card would if you were at a hotel and attempting to get into your room. This will also hold your tab if you have any drinks at the bar or dine in our restaurant. The attendant will simply scan the band, and it will charge you an invoice, which will charge your credit card at the end of the night."

"Oh, I love this," Jenna says as she rubs her hands together like a villain ready to take down the world.

"One more thing. Here are your bags. Please place any personal effects such as cell phones, ID cards or credit cards, and keys in here."

She hands us each a black velvet bag with a deep red drawstring. The fabric is cool and luxurious to the touch, as it should be for the monthly price of this place. I toss my belongings in and wait for Jenna to do the same.

"To ensure their protection, these items will be placed in a safe deposit box. When you're ready to leave, make a stop here, and I'll scan your bracelet to retrieve your belongings. The club is right through that door. Would you like a tour?" Jenna and I both shake our heads. I think we'll manage just fine. "Well then, we at Obsidian hope you both enjoy your night," she says as she walks to another door and leaves Jenna and me.

"Thanks, you too," I say without thinking.

"Thanks, you too?" Jenna laughs. "What's she supposed to enjoy out here?"

"Shut up, I'm nervous!" I say, opening the door she pointed to on the left.

A few short steps forward and we find ourselves in a room filled with an exquisite arrangement of black, red, and white fabric spanning from the floor to the ceiling. The room is filled with a chaotic dance of red and white light beams, forming mesmerizing geometric shapes. As the lights hit the glitter marble floors, they are transformed into a mesmerizing canvas of rainbow hues.

Plush velvet couches are scattered throughout the enormous room, some in dark, secluded corners for privacy and others which appear strategically placed for an audience.

The bar beckons us with its crimson lighting, casting an alluring hue and showcasing shelves brimming with bottles that seem to scrape the ceiling. Massive disco balls adorn its high ceilings, suspended at varying heights, casting an enchanting array of sparkles that captivate my attention.

"This place is gorgeous. Whoever owns it did an amazing job," I yell over the music. "You wouldn't expect this from the outside."

"Are you saying you're glad I brought you?" she asks with knowing eyes. I'm a sucker for anything interior design. If I wasn't meant to follow in my dad's footsteps, I could see myself being an interior designer, creating beautiful spaces like this.

"Possibly." I smirk and give her a shrug.

"Good, because you need this, Lex. If it was up to you, you'd be in your bed reading your latest book about couples who don't exist. Guys who don't exist."

"Hey, hey, hey, don't bring my books into this," I say, feigning defensiveness.

"Fine. But you know I'm right."

"You are, and to show my appreciation," I say as I eye the bartender heading our way, "I'll buy the first round of drinks."

After ordering my go-to vodka cranberry and Jenna's classic martini, we move to the dance floor.

After three more drinks and a dozen songs, I'm in desperate need of a break and some air. This leather dress clings to the skin in the most uncomfortable way. I discreetly blow air down my cleavage in hopes it will cool me down.

Glancing to the left, I see Jenna dancing with some guy, their movements so close and intimate. It's hard to tell where the dancing ends and something more begins. I swear she's like a magnet for all guys, where I'm more of a repellant.

I catch her eye and communicate my need to visit the restroom. With a thumbs-up from her, I make my way toward the bathrooms. Wherever they are.

My eyes search for any sign that might indicate their whereabouts. There aren't any. Maybe we should have taken the receptionist up on the tour.

Taking a gamble, I opt to go toward the first door I come across on the right-hand side. I hold my bracelet over the small screen, and it turns red. The door's lock clicks before swinging open, revealing an empty hallway equally as breathtaking as the rest of this place. Okay... that's kind of cool.

Shattered floor-to-ceiling mirrors create a mosaic of a million fragmented pieces, yet somehow remain intact as a kaleidoscope of colors form as the light dances along the walls.

The hallway turns left, leading me to yet another door. As I walk toward it, my eyes are drawn to a table adorned with a basket overflowing with vibrant masquerade masks. A sign politely instructs visitors to don a mask before proceeding.

I turn around in the empty hallway and wonder if I should head back the way I came. With a mix of curiosity and uncertainty, I decide to put on the mask and cautiously turn the knob on the door. Jenna's earlier words of living a little propel me forward. What's the worst that can happen?

As I walk in, I come to an abrupt halt.

The room is spacious but devoid of light besides floor lighting, like in a movie theater along the baseboards. There are large windows on every wall. Some people also donning masks are curiously peering into those windows. While others seem five seconds away from fucking in the middle of the room where more comfy-looking couches are situated.

What the hell did I just stumble into?

I clutch the mask tightly, ensuring it won't slip off. The screams in my mind fade into the background as I wear the mask, giving me the courage to move forward, empowered by the anonymity that shrouds me.

No feelings of embarrassment or guilt run through me as they usually do when I'm watching porn. It's refreshing and freeing.

With caution, I quickly glance through the first window. A shiver runs down my spine, my breath hitching in my throat as I find myself frozen, unable to tear my gaze away.

A woman is strapped to an enormous piece of wood in the shape of an X in the middle of the room. The room is decked out in some medieval-looking torture chamber shit. Bricks adorn the walls, giving the effect of a genuine dungeon.

Hundreds of flickering candles illuminate the room, casting a soft and mysterious glow on the walls, displaying various whips and paddles. The man in the room is naked besides his black leather mask. He whips the woman on different parts of her body, making her scream in ecstasy and beg for more. My eyes widen in shock. This is unlike anything I've ever seen. I've read about it, yes, even fantasized about it a time or two, but witnessing it firsthand is a whole new experience.

My heart pounds in my chest as I let what I see wash over me, making a powerful sensation reach my core. A spark of intrigue has ignited within me, and I never want the excitement to fade.

I take one last glance at the woman strapped down before making my way to the next window.

The next room resembles an exam room at a doctor's office, with sterile white walls and a bright overhead light. A busty nurse in a candy striper costume with a stethoscope around her neck stands over a naked woman on the exam table. The nurse takes a metal instrument and rolls it down the woman's body as she writhes on the table. As she goes between the woman's legs, she rolls the instrument against her most sensitive flesh, making her scream. Which makes more viewers crowd the window. I take that as my cue to head to the next room.

A few people occupy the next window. The interior is a weathered, Gothic-style church, where the ethereal glow of stained glass bathes the space in a mesmerizing display of colors. A man in black clothing and a white collar stands over a young woman kneeling at his feet, dressed in only a plaid skirt, white ruffle socks, and chunky patent leather Mary Janes. He speaks to her while rubbing her head. She nods at whatever he says before a slow smile plays on her red-painted lips. The man grabs the woman's hand, and they walk into the confessional that's off to the right and out of sight.

Catholicism was a big part of growing up in the families. Another way to wash all the bloody hands—confessional on Saturday followed by Eucharist on Sunday just to murder on Monday. The teachings have made a lasting impression, and as a result, this scene is profoundly unsettling, but what's truly alarming is how captivated I am by it.

The fourth room is an enormous cage that looks to be two stories high, with a mattress at the bottom and dozens of silk pillows. No one is inside, and I'm almost disappointed. I'm curious about what happens in this room.

As I approach the last window, I have to lean in against the glass and squint to make out what's inside.

A chaotic swirl of vibrant graffiti explodes across the walls, the only visible shapes in the overwhelmingly dark room, set off by the flashing black lights and strobes, creating a rhythmic, pulsing light show. A brightly painted couple moves into my view and sways to the thumping bass of house music emanating from the room. The lights flicker in perfect synchrony with the music's rhythm. It's reminiscent of a wild, pulsating rave.

As I observe the scene, I notice a second man positioned discreetly behind the first man who is grabbing the woman. Their actions have me fixated, unable to avert my gaze. They move to the music and explore each other's bodies unhurriedly, with each touch eliciting a euphoric expression.

Out of nowhere, a fiery sensation surges through my body, starting from my spine and working its way up my nape. Without warning, an imposing figure appears behind me and forcefully pushes their body into mine.

And what do I do? Nothing.

The mix of shock and a touch of arousal leaves me bewildered.

When I raise my eyes, I'm instantly fascinated by their hands and fingers, covered in elaborate tattoos and embellished with rings on their middle and pinky fingers, which lean against the cold glass window.

Something about this person's presence is incredibly powerful, almost overwhelming.

His other hand scrapes down my left side, leaving a trail of fire in its wake. Then, he grabs my waist with a rough grip, and I can't help but gasp in surprise. He brings me even further back against him and angles my hips so my ass is rubbing against his extremely hard crotch.

To steady myself, I press both palms against the window. He moves me back and forth a few times to show me just how hard he is while holding me securely, like I might disappear.

As a surge of excitement and fear rushes through me, a moan escapes my lips involuntarily.

I feel the soft brush of a beard against my ear as he leans into me, followed by the most deliciously deep and raspy voice I've ever heard.

"Do you like what you've seen tonight, piccolo angello? Do you wish it was you in one of these rooms getting worshipped by a man who's been starved for an eternity?"

Even in the face of my silence, he carries on with his words.

"Do you see the way they're touching her?" He asks as he sniffs along my neck, leaving goosebumps in his wake. "That is but a mere taste of what I'd do to you. How I'd own every piece of you, one by one, until all you remember is me and me alone." His words continue to flow smoothly and with a sense of certainty.

He's unhurried and confident.

Yet his sharp and cutting words pierce through me in all the right ways, leaving me weak and yearning.

What is happening to me and why do I like it so much?

Before I'm able to reply, a satisfied chuckle reaches my ear, followed by sweet pain as he bites my earlobe.

Hard.

A sudden, unexpected squeal escapes my lips, followed by another zap to my core, which blends surprise with a profound yearning for him to do it again.

My legs give out as his grip tightens.

He's holding me together, while simultaneously causing me to fall apart.

A wave of intense heat washes over me, as if the sun itself has suddenly shifted closer. My body is flushed from head to toe. My dress is practically suffocating.

Maybe I will take Jenna's advice and let him rip the damn thing to shreds.

This sweet madness he's creating in me feels like a delicious poison, a captivating destruction.

I could blame it on the drinks in my system, but I know it's not that.

It's him.

It's the power I feel radiating off him as he grabs and takes, his controlling tone, and his air of dominance. All things that would usually send me running, but now leave me with a strange, insatiable desire for more.

Five

Gage

Six years and eleven months—that's how long I've anticipated this very moment.

I've fantasized about this exact moment for many more.

This woman has had a fucking chokehold on me since I was a boy.

From sunrise to sunset, she occupies my mind as both my first and last thought.

The cherry on top of this delicious fucked-up cake is that she doesn't even know it's me.

I knew she'd never come here on her own, so I had Jace, my friend and head of security, go to her friend Jenna's place of work. He flashed his smile at one of the dancers, then invited her here for a night of fun. She, of course, went back to Jenna and the other dancers, eager to relay the information she had no right giving since she signed the NDA. Usually, that would piss me the fuck off, but it was my only shot at getting Alexa here, and it worked.

It fucking worked.

One day soon, she'll realize who is touching her and who she belongs to.

Who she's always belonged to.

Until then, I'm going to take full advantage of this moment.

As she and her friend made their way through the club, I observed her intently, my instincts sharpened like a wolf poised to strike.

I made sure no fucker touched her or even got in her vicinity, just as I've done since getting out of prison.

Ever since she left college and my brother Marco, I've thwarted every attempt toward her. Some guys bowed out gracefully, others, not so much. The thought of someone touching her sends waves of fury coursing through my veins.

Jace is responsible for babysitting her friend tonight, leaving the little lamb all by herself.

Never did I think she'd venture into The Viewing Room. A favorite of the patrons.

They pay a pretty penny to have an exclusive monthly membership beyond the bar and club, to act out their darkest desires and fantasies. There's nothing wrong with embarking on a journey of self-discovery and exploring the depths of others, and that's precisely what I intend to do with Alexa.

I followed her through one of the many secret doors I had added when I was overseeing the build. My top priority is having an escape route, so I never feel trapped like a fucking animal again.

I click the false panel and walk through as I adjust my mask. This is the perfect opportunity to make my presence known, but anonymously.

I watch her like prey, making her rounds to each window. Observing her breathing grow shallower as she watches the debauchery makes me lightheaded. She likes what she sees. Her eyes are filled with curiosity and desire, and as she repeatedly licks her pink pillowy lips, my excitement grows.

I count to ten, trying to regain my composure, aware that we have an eternity together, though I'm tired of waiting.

Anger wells inside me as I notice a guy leering at her all by herself. I take it as my signal to step toward her, my gaze piercing into him, silently conveying my message to fuck off.

The closer I get to her, the more strongly I sense the ever-present, enigmatic force pulling us together, an undeniable connection that's always existed. The need to touch her, get under her skin, and consume her. I couldn't stop myself even if I wanted to. The demand, a hot, urgent thrumming, pulses through my veins, screaming for attention.

The moment I push my front into her back, I sense her body stiffen in surprise. I want her to remember how close we were, how good we could have been. How good we will be.

She has always fit me perfectly, and now it feels like a missing puzzle piece finally sliding into place as we come together again.

As I lean in, her candy-coated coconut scent fills my senses. I close my eyes and reminisce. Countless memories flood my thoughts. Laughter, happiness, and unrequited love.

She's mine. My fantasy, my dream girl, my everything.

I slowly trail my hand up her spine before winding my fingers into the soft black hair at her nape. With the heels she's in, the top of her head barely reaches my chin, but it's the perfect height for me to devour her. With a slight tug, I move her head to the left, exposing her vulnerable neck. I sniff and suck from her jawline

41

down to her collarbone, eliciting goose bumps from her sensitive skin.

She's so responsive; putty in my hands. So attuned to the way I touch her.

Right now, I think she's willing to do almost anything. I decide to push her even further, not able to resist the temptation.

I remove my other hand from the window, bringing it to her abdomen and descending. The moment I arrive at the junction between her thighs, I close my eyes to fully experience the warmth and the sounds she is creating exclusively for me.

My fingers trace a small circle against her clit, pressing harder and moving faster with each rotation. She's drenched, and through the buzzing in my ears and her muted sounds, I can still envision the sound of her wetness based on the sensation of her moisture on my fingers.

It would be so easy to make her come but I want her on edge. I want her to beg me for more.

Just as I feel her getting close, I back off.

"Oh God, please don't stop," she whimpers.

A smirk reaches my lips. "Now, now, piccolo angello. You'll have plenty of time to beg me," I say against her ear with a triumphant smile before rubbing her again with hard strokes.

Right now, having her under my dominance is the most freeing and exhilarating sensation I've experienced since leaving prison almost two years ago.

As I glance to my left, I notice a small group of people observing our every move. It's time to take her to a secluded place, away from prying eyes.

I enjoy voyeurism, but not when it comes to the eyes being on her.

No one but me will witness her begging, pleading, or screaming.

No one will witness the way she falls apart except for me.

"Come with me," I coax while pulling her away from the window and toward the door.

I want to feel her fear and see her run.

"Alexa!" someone says from behind me, and I go stiff. *Shit, her friend.* I should have disabled her bracelet the second I followed Alexa in here.

We both turn toward the unwelcome noise.

Her friend's timing fucking sucks.

Six

Alexa

I turn toward Jenna, who's looking a little disheveled and buzzed as hell with glossy, bloodshot eyes.

"Are you okay?" I ask, stepping closer to her.

"Are you almost ready to go?" she says, scanning our surroundings.

I most definitely am not ready to go. I'm five seconds away from having one of the best all-consuming orgasms of my life, and then this happens. If I didn't have shit luck, I wouldn't have any luck at all.

"Just give me a second," I say as I glance back at my mystery guy... who isn't there?

What the fuck?

Where did he go? What a prick.

Unless I imagined him in a drunken haze. Which would be terrifying—and something I should speak to Dr. Schults about.

Looking back at Jenna, I shrug. "Let's go."

I interlock my arm with hers and walk with her out the door, through the kaleidoscope hallway, and into the bar area.

I try to avoid searching for my mystery guy, who may or may not be real. Not that I'd have much to go on besides tattooed hands and built like a brick wall.

Once we gather our belongings, including my switchblade, which I attach to my body right away, we exit through the front entrance. A rush of refreshing, cool air compels me to take a long, satisfying breath in, and then out, to purge my mind and body of all the debauchery that pumped through my veins minutes ago.

"Keys." I hold my hand out to Jenna, and she hands them over without a fight before climbing into the passenger side.

I make my way around to the driver's side, but halt when I see another red rose hanging from the driver's-side door handle.

A wave of nausea hits me as my stomach plummets and I frantically scan the dark, deserted parking lot.

Now I'm a little creeped out, thinking someone followed us. I throw it on the concrete, hurry inside the car, and slam the door lock.

Once I'm on the freeway, the tension eases as I glance in the rearview mirror and see no signs of anyone following us.

I turn my attention to Jenna, who's curled up on her side. "You sure you're okay? Do you want to talk about it?" I say just above a whisper.

It's a rare occurrence for her to be in this state. Mostly, she's a ball of sunshine. Her infectious energy lights up the room, but every so often, a wave of melancholy washes over her.

She avoids discussions about her past, but I sense it sometimes affects her. I mean, how could it not? She's an orphan. The thought of not having my family is unbearable, and I hate that she only has me, that she never had a dad to protect her and a mom to love her unconditionally.

"I'm good, I promise," she mumbles.

"I'm always here if you want to talk. You know that, right?" I ask, giving her back a rub.

"Yeah."

After we get home, I make sure Jenna gets in her place safely, then head to mine. I take my shears to the too tight dress and moan in satisfaction as it falls to the floor, then hop in the shower. The thought of sinking into my soft sheets and sleeping for a solid three to five business days is all I can think about as I rush through my night routine.

My mind drifts back to earlier at the club. I still can't believe that guy. He acted like he wanted to devour me whole. Only to ghost me the second my back was turned.

I rub my hand against my side where his fingers traveled. He had to be real. I can still smell him, still feel him. How his hands grabbed hold of me. Anchoring me to him. How his fingers worked me.

Guiding me to the highest peaks. And how his words caressed me. Mind, body, and soul.

Only to leave me hanging.

What a dick.

"We came, we saw, we conquered. Can we go home now?" I say with a huff as I wind my hair into a bun, which should be criminal since I just got a fresh blowout. I'm exhausted from last night, and Jenna woke me up at the ass crack of dawn for a massage, which was actually just my body getting polished and waxed until I'm raw and shiny but hydrated. Followed by shopping.

"Not until we eat. I'm starving. What are you feeling like? Italian? Mediterranean?"

Honestly, I will have anything if it gets us home sooner.

"You decide." I yawn. "I'm not feeling picky today."

"Shocker," she says and gestures with her palms to her mouth.

"I am not picky!"

"Oh yes, you are. You're picky with food and men."

"I find those both reasonable things to be picky about."

"Eh, true. But still. The way you're going, you'll end up dying a virgin who has the food variety of a child. I think we'll have Mediterranean. Let's go." She all but pulls me to a little restaurant down the street.

The inside is adorable. Different shades of green. Plants and mosaic Turkish chandeliers hang from the ceiling, giving the whole restaurant an intimate, upscale tree-house vibe. We opt for a patio seat since the weather is so nice.

"What did you think of the club last night?" Jenna asks with a mouthful of falafel.

"It was okay. The music was decent, and the drinks were lethal. Wouldn't you say?" I say, poking fun at how drunk she was and steering the conversation away from the sex room I was held hostage in before getting ghosted.

"Indeed. There was none of that watered-down shit like I make at the strip club."

"So did you get that guy's number or..."

"Of course. I told him we'd be back soon. Real soon," she says as she does a little happy dance.

I shake my head. "Once was more than enough for me."

"Oh no you don't. You had fun, and we both know it." She points a finger in my face. "That guy, Jace, I think his name was, says the front area is only like twenty percent of the entire club. Can you believe that shit?" Her eyes are wide with disbelief.

"Do you remember coming to get me? In the back, in that other room," I ask vaguely as I take my beef kebab and dunk it into hummus.

"Barely. I was trashed." She shrugs.

"You didn't see the guy with me?"

She squints like she's trying to remember. "I think I saw a guy's back, but not much else."

Well, at least I didn't imagine him.

My phone ringing startles me and I see the caller ID flash with an unknown number before reluctantly answering.

"Lex," Rosie says from the other end. Her voice causes my back to snap straight.

"Oh my fucking God. I thought something happened to you. Why haven't you answered any of my calls or texts?"

"I broke my phone when I fell out my window." I laugh as I imagine her hanging from the trellis outside her window at her parents' house. "Not funny. It hurt like hell."

"Maybe a little funny," I say with a smile. "Are you okay? Where did you end up, anyway?"

"A small town on the border of Illinois and Indiana."

I quirk a brow. "But I thought..."

"I got intercepted."

Intercepted?

"What the hell does that mean?"

Rosie pauses, and the silence stretches, making me worry we lost the connection. Then she speaks, uttering the one sentence I never expected her to say.

"Gage found me."

With a creak, my back meets the chair while my mouth hangs open and my eyes widen in disbelief. I'm unable to form a sentence, let alone a word for Rosie, or even Jenna, whose face shows concern. My stomach is in my throat, and it seems the world has stopped moving.

"Hello?" Rosie asks.

"He-he's back?" I say as I swallow down the lump in my throat.

"Yeah, and he's not the same."

"What do you mean?"

"Imagine him from before. Honest. Sweet. Understanding. Now throw that version in the trash. He turned into a hard man, Lex. You can see the ruthlessness in his eyes, but he did hit one of the guards over the head to knock him out cold to save me, so maybe he's not all bad."

Jenna's hands go up in question, and I mouth to her, "Gage is back."

I can't wrap my mind around Gage being back. I want to ask her a million questions. What does he look like now? Does he still have that same smile, where his upper lip subtly tilts upward as if he's attempting to hide his delight? Where has he been? How is he doing? But what screams in my head the most is why did he find her and still leave me behind? It's not a jealousy thing because he's her brother. I'm glad she has him back. I'm just heartbroken and feel insignificant. But I don't ask those questions or tell her the way I feel because my heart hurts too much to know the answer.

So I move the conversation from him and ask about the guard.

"Which one?"

"Alfonso."

"No way."

"Yeah, he had blood trickling from his head while he was lying on the ground. I even got to kick him in the ribs on the way out."

A mischievous smile tugs at the corners of my mouth as I think about my best friend, who is usually so gentle, engaging in an act of violence. "You should have kicked him in the balls so he's unable to procreate. He always gave me the creeps with his leering and weird comments about our clothes."

"For real. Maybe next time."

"Who are you, and what have you done with my best friend? First, running away, and then violence... Please tell me you've already made two horrible decisions but regret nothing."

"I haven't been able to do shit since Gage happened."

"So he's really back?" I ask with tears lining my eyes.

"Yep. Just be thankful you haven't run into him yet."

"Yeah, I guess so," I say with a resigned sigh. "So where are you staying? With him?"

"No, he dropped me off at some friend's house who is now my babysitter."

My heart beats painfully as I think about him with someone. "A girl?"

Jenna's eyebrow raises, and I feel like an idiot for voicing the question aloud.

"No. A dick. I swear he makes me want to poke out his eyeballs."

Relief fills me, and I feel like a hypocrite, considering some unknown guy's hands were all over me not even twenty-four hours ago.

"Is he cute?" I ask.

"No, he's ugly as hell and a total asshole. I mean, I get he's helping me out, or more like helping Gage out, but fuck, is he irritating. I don't want to talk about me, though. Tell me about you. Are you okay?"

"I'm good, Ro. Real good. You'd like it here." Silence greets me on the other end. "Hey, you still there?"

"Yeah, sorry," she says, sounding preoccupied.

A hand appears in front of my face to place our baklava we ordered for dessert. I glance upward, offering a silent thank you and a smile to the server.

"Can we talk tomorrow? They just delivered our dessert."

"Yeah. Love you, Lex."

"Love you, Ro," I say as I hang up and place my phone on the table before gazing at Jenna.

"Maybe Gage is just doing his rounds, and you're next," she says, her expression hopeful. She doesn't know him, but I've talked about him more than enough times on a drunken night when I was in my feelings.

My mind goes to the saying, 'If he wanted to, he would.'

I clear the emotion in my throat. "It's fine. I need to focus on myself."

"Let's go back to the club, then," she says as she wags her eyebrows.

"You—"

"Good evening. Your tab has been taken care of for the night. We hope you enjoyed yourselves," the server says before bowing his head and walking away.

"Well, shit, lucky us," Jenna says, rising from her seat and grabbing her bags.

"Yeah, sure," I say, looking around. "Nothing is ever free in this world," I say more to myself just as my phone buzzes.

Unknown

> Little Lamb, little lamb, where have you been?

The gravelly texture of his deep voice, like stones scraping against each other, is so present in my mind that a gasp escapes me, and a flutter stirs deep within my core.

What the fuck?

Alexa

> How the hell did you get my number?

Unknown

> You'd be surprised at what I'm capable of when there's something I want.

Alexa

> Says The Ghoster

Unknown

> Make no mistake, you were never ghosted. I've kept tabs on you.

Alexa

> Sounds like I need to take out a restraining order.

Unknown

> Restraining you would please me much more.

I roll my eyes and pocket my phone. He's pretty ballsy. I'll give him that.

Once home, I hang all my new outfits up, then lie on my bed. I'm exhausted.

Bing. A notification.

Unknown

Leaving me on read... what bad manners you have.

Alexa

Says the guy who vanished. Why don't you take a hike? I'm not interested.

Unknown

See me again.

Alexa

Not a chance in hell. Go find someone else to annoy and waste their time.

Who does this guy think he is? Like I'm just going to fall at his feet.

Unknown

Oh, you thought I was asking...? This isn't a request.

I roll my eyes and leave him on read again.

He might have magic fingers and a voice dripping with so much sexual intent I'm putty in his hands, but I'm not interested.

I learned my lesson with Marco. He remained cold and distant until something came over him, and he changed, making me believe we had a real chance to make things work. Then I walked in on him with a girl's face buried in his lap.

Seven

Alexa

10 MONTHS AGO-20 YEARS OLD

Rosie and I stare at our newly decorated dorm room. Rosie's side is a mix of pretty pastels, while I prefer the darker hues of blacks and greens. It's like a colorful sunset to a dark storm. You can definitely tell which side is whose.

"I can't believe this is our life now, questionable decisions, parties galore—"

"Not for long," Rosie says with a sigh.

"Don't you dare ruin this monumental moment, Rosalinda," I say as I hip check her. She had a fight with her father right before we left. He almost changed his mind and wouldn't let her come. I don't understand why he always has to be so hard on her, on all his kids.

With my dad's help, he finally agreed, and we took off like a shot, exceeding the speed limit a few times because we couldn't bear to miss a single second of our newly earned freedom.

It took a year of begging our parents before they both relented and allowed us a year of college. We took some courses online after high school, accounting for me and dance and art for Rosie, but it wasn't enough. I wanted this experience, and so did Rosie. Better late than never, I guess.

"I'm hungry. Do you want to go check out the town and see what we can find?"

"Yeah, sounds good to me. I'm starving."

We decide to try a bar and grill around the corner from the university she heard about from one of the other girls in our dorm while she was checking out the shower situation.

It didn't take long to locate the place once we stepped foot outside our dorm. The pounding rhythm of the music echoed through the streets, leading us straight to it.

We follow a group of people around our age down a set of stairs. My mind is blown. The bar is in a basement?

"This place is kind of awesome," Rosie yells in my ear.

"Agreed," I say with a nod.

My dad would have a coronary. He would consider this highly unsafe, and I can almost envision his protest. What if there's a fire, Alexandria? What if there's a shooter? Where's your way out? Did you bring your gun?

I survey my surroundings and notice a sign against the back wall with an emergency exit highlighted in red neon lights over the top, then I discreetly rub my fingertips against my jean skirt-covered thigh to feel for the handle to my blade. Hopefully, that will chill my dad's voice out in my head and calm my nerves.

As we hit the bottom step, I see a dozen pool tables off to the right-hand side. A huge collage of TVs sit on the wall along the left side where a music video is playing. There's a stage where it looks like a band is setting up. Everything is dark, and I kind of love it.

I can get used to this. I smile to myself before I get pulled toward the bar to order.

Once we're done ordering, we sit and observe.

"Do you want to play pool after we eat?"

"As long as you keep the jokes to a minimum. I still suck," I say with a pout. I'm competitive, and I hate losing, which is what I do frequently while playing pool.

When I'd go to her house, we'd play in the game room. It was always her and me against Gage and Marco. The guys would unfortunately always win, which was no fault of Rosie's, always mine. Poor Rosie would have to deal with a dare for losing.

One time we had to jump in the pool in the dead of winter. It was brutal. I thought I was going to shiver the skin off my bones, and my dad almost strangled the guys for the stupid dare.

"Now's the time to work on it so we can kick both Gage's and Marco's asses," I say with a determined smile.

"You think we'll ever hear from Gage again?" Rosie asks, frowning.

"I used to say yes, but I don't know anymore."

Gage got out almost a year ago, and we still haven't heard from him. He disappeared without a trace. Just walked out the door of Metro Correctional Center on his release day and poof, gone.

To this day, I miss him. The day he went away felt like a piece of my heart got ripped out of my chest. I mourned him that day and every day since.

He was just as important as Rosie was to me. Maybe more so in some ways. He gave the best hugs, the ones you felt in your soul. The kind you never wanted to end, like holding a lifeline. And his smile. His smile was magical and always made his deep-blue eyes sparkle like the sun hitting the sea.

We get our food and dig in. Rosie ordered their loaded nachos while I chose the boring chicken strips and fries. It's the safest thing on the menu, and I know there won't be any surprises. I've had an aversion to sauces and extra flavors on food my whole life. Sometimes less is more, and that can be said for many things.

I finish mine in record time and look up at Rosie, who's also done. We grab our drinks and head over to an empty table to play. It takes more coordination than I have, but I'm getting better. Soon, we finish one game. She wins, of course, and racks the balls to start another game.

"Mind if I join?" a deep voice asks from behind me.

"Aw man, how'd you find us, Marco?" Rosie asks.

I turn around and see the body attached to the voice. Handsome in a boy-next-door type of way with short dark brown hair and light blue eyes. He's tall and lean because of sports. He stands with a confidence about him that's infectious and makes me want to lean closer.

I haven't seen him since he started attending the college Rosie and I are now also attending. He's making this his final year before diving into the family business with the rest of us, and I hope to grow closer to him before that happens. Dad told me the marriage contract between our families was signed, so he and I are a done deal.

"I'm always looking out for my girls." His grin makes me smile, while Rosie scrunches up her nose like she smells something awful.

"Don't look too closely. I want to have fun while I'm here," Rosie says.

Her father gave her one year of college before she goes back to marry Manuel. She still hasn't warmed up to the idea, and I don't blame her.

We decide to play another game. Two against one since he thinks he can smoke us both.

It's my turn, and I totally miss the ball.

"Can I help?" Marco asks.

I'm not sure how he's going to help since he's never offered before, but I say yes anyway. I can't help but feel curious and slightly pleased by his attention. It's a welcome change from his usual brush-off.

He tells me to line the stick up to the ball, and I do. I'm bent over the table when I feel him behind me, bending with me and putting his hands over mine.

My eyes widen, but I don't dare to raise my gaze toward Rosie. I'm sure I'm about as red as a tomato.

Marco is leaning on top of me. He whispers in my ear exactly how I need to hold the stick, then helps me take the shot. It goes right into the pocket, and I jump up, giving him a high five, and then Rosie.

That was intense. I take a huge breath to compose myself before I turn back toward him and thank him. He gives me a smile and a brief nod.

We play for another hour, then decide to head back to the dorm. Marco walks us back since he deems it unsafe, for which I'm grateful.

Rosie and I have heard horror stories about walking alone at night through college campuses. Mainly from our parents being overprotective, but I still heed their warnings, and after that one night after my swim meet, I've been extra cautious.

We *never found the white van that stopped in front of me the night I was run off the road. The guy who Dad killed belonged to a disgruntled local gang who disagreed with a certain decision, and they set their sights on me. The scar that stretches from the corner of my eyebrow to the top of my ear serves as a constant tingling reminder of the consequences of my carelessness. I need to stay vigilant and ready but still live life, which feels like a battle I'm never going to conquer.*

We walk into the building to our dorm, Rosie first, when Marco grabs my hand to stop me.

"Go on up, Rosie. Alexa will be up in a minute. We're just going to have a quick chat."

My heart stops. What does he want to talk about?

"Okay, but be nice," Rosie says, narrowing her eyes at her brother.

"Aren't I always?"

"No. And she's mine until your stupid arranged marriage," she says as she rolls her eyes and keeps walking.

"I had fun tonight," Marco says, avoiding the talk of our arranged marriage.

"Yeah, me too. Thanks for the help playing," I say lamely.

Why do I always have to be so awkward?

"No problem. I don't mind helping a damsel in distress," he says while squeezing my hand that I just realized he's still holding.

My gaze falls to our intertwined hands until he gently lifts my chin.

The next thing I know, he's leaning in for a kiss.

My breath catches in my throat.

Oh my gosh. It's happening.

At the last minute, he gives me one on my cheek and steps back, letting my hand go.

"Good night, Alexa," he says before turning around and walking away.

"Good night," I say to his back.

I watch his retreating form until it's blocked by the guys' dorms, then I turn around and head inside.

What the heck was that? Was he actually going to kiss me, or was I imagining it?

When I get to my room, Rosie is already in bed. I pull out my pajamas to get more comfortable.

"Marco is too much sometimes."

"True that. I think he'll leave us alone after a week or two," I say, not wanting to discuss the almost kiss with her.

She's my best friend, and I also consider her my sister, but it's weird talking to her about her brother, no matter what the plans for the future may be.

✦

The months in college pass quickly. We're busy with classes and having as much fun as possible while still trying to cram sleep in somewhere.

Marco hangs out with us sometimes when he's not busy. We have yet to discuss the night of the almost kiss. He also hasn't tried to get close to me since then, either.

Maybe he's just not interested, or maybe my mind made more of it than there was? All I know is that it will make for an unpleasant situation later on if we don't figure this out.

It's Friday, and we're planning on heading to a party off campus at one of Marco's college friend's houses.

Rosie begged him, and he relented with a couple of rules we must follow. We agreed, and that sealed the deal.

It's themed Devils and Angels night, which I find silly, but I'm not going to turn down my first college party.

We're decked out in flowy dresses that hit a couple of inches above our knees. Rosie in white, me in black. Angel wings are strapped to our backs, and the cutest little halo crowns I made with fake flowers and zip ties spray painted gold that are pointed to the heavens.

We both gaze in the mirror, smiling at each other. We look good.

There's a knock on our door and Marco strolls in, looking wicked in his devil costume. Black slacks hang from this narrow waist with a red silk shirt and a cape. He even has little red horns on his mask and a pitchfork.

He looks at both of us for a few seconds. "No."

"Please, Marco. Our outfits took forever, and we're already ready," Rosie pleads and pushes out her bottom lip for good measure.

I do the same when he just stays silent, watching us, and then I get an idea.

I get on my knees, clasping my hands together above my head. "Pretty please, I promise we'll be good," I say.

"No way I'm kneeling before him," Rosie grumbles.

He looks down at me and gives me a little smirk before looking out the window. "Fine, let's go," he says as he turns toward the door.

We get to the party about twenty minutes later. The house is massive. It's white with four immense columns that alternate in red and black lighting, creating an ominous effect.

From the outside, the thumping music is audible. I'm buzzing with excitement. My first actual party.

As we make our way up the steps, he stops and reminds us to stick by him, don't accept drinks from anyone, and so on.

The moment the doors open, it looks like a bomb went off. People are everywhere, and red cups litter every surface. A thick layer of smoke is in the air, muting the colorful flashing lights. It's a little crazier than what I expected.

We weave through crowds of people, and I feel a hand grab mine. I glance downward and see it's Marco's. He avoids my gaze as we move through the house. We stop near the kitchen and Rosie sees a friend from art class she wants to say hi to. He hesitates, then tells her to return swiftly, his voice laced with apprehension. A roll of her eyes, a light skip, and she's gone.

It's then I realize I'm left by myself with him. I glance around, unsure of what I'm supposed to do. When I look back at him, he's staring at me.

"I'll be back. I have to check something," he says before walking away without a second glance.

"Okay..." I stand around awkwardly, not knowing anyone. I'm not a social butterfly, and I don't like crowds. I wish the wall would swallow me up.

Seconds later, he's back at my side.

"That was quick." I smile over at him, relieved not to be alone.

"You want to go out back?" He nods toward the back door, a small smirk playing on his lips.

"Sure," I say embarrassingly quick.

He grabs my hand again and pulls me toward the door, then out onto the back patio.

Red twinkle lights cast a warm and enchanting glow, transforming the backyard into a captivating oasis. Tons of people are swimming and in all stages of undress.

To the right, a firepit crackles with warmth. Multiple people are gathered around, drinking and toasting marshmallows.

He leads me toward the left side of the yard, the faint scent of flowers growing stronger. We descend a few stairs and arrive at a secluded area with a well-tended garden.

"Thanks for letting us come tonight. Rosie was so excited," I say while looking up at the sky, although I'm aware his eyes are on me.

"Everything was worth it after seeing you in this. You look gorgeous."

I smile, then feel him place his hand on my hip before giving it a little squeeze. Surprise has my stomach plunging, and I inhale sharply. A surge of giddy anticipation washes over me as our gazes meet.

His sudden forwardness is confusing to me, given that he has shown no interest in me during our past few weeks of spending time together or at any point before.

I don't know what changed, but I'm glad it did. Maybe this will work after all.

As he pulls me closer, the atmosphere becomes charged with energy. We're now chest to chest, and his gloved hands are grabbing the sides of my face. His lips are so tempting that I can't help but imagine how they would feel against mine.

The devious grin adorning his face has nothing to do with his current costume, as he catches me staring at him.

His head tilts down toward mine, deviating from the expected cheek kiss. The anticipation makes my palms sweat, and butterflies consume my stomach.

His lips brush against mine in a soft kiss that leaves me moaning for another. His tongue runs against my lips, asking for entrance to my mouth. I open it slowly and he takes full advantage, plunging his tongue in. It's warm, soft, and intoxicating.

Much better than any taste of alcohol. It makes my head dizzy with delight.

I get lost in my first kiss.

I cling to him as he holds me afloat and keeps me from drifting away like a boat without an anchor on a stormy night.

We kiss for what seems like hours, but it is only a few brief minutes before he pulls away. His forehead rests against mine as we catch our breath and it gives me a flashback to a different time.

With Gage.

Guilt washes over me the instant my mind goes there. This isn't fair to Marco, especially now that he's trying and showing interest in me.

As I open my eyes, I'm met with his piercing gaze. He leans in and captures my lips once more before pulling me back to the party. I'm a little dazed, but so damn happy.

Eight

Alexa

I wake with a start.

The curtain from my sliding glass door billows in the chilly early morning wind.

Did I leave it open last night? No, I don't think I did.

As I scan my room, a shiver runs down my spine, and it has nothing to do with the air rushing into my room.

I'm not alone.

I shriek when I see something from the corner of my eye, but the shadow is on me in seconds.

A warm palm covers my mouth, making it impossible to make any noise. The sweet and spicy scent of cologne hits me in waves and reminds me of who it is and the first time we met.

"Shhh, Little Lamb. It's only me."

"What the fuck are you doing in my house?" I say, muffled, as he still hasn't removed his hand from my mouth.

This motherfucker is getting slapped with a restraining order for sure now.

He jumps on top of me, effectively caging me in with each strong thighs while squeezing my legs together and pinning me down with some of his weight. His other hand holds both of mine above my head, rendering me immobile while his face is mere inches from mine.

"I'm going to remove my hand. If you scream, I'll resort to harsher methods. Methods I'll enjoy greatly, but you probably won't. It's entirely up to you."

"Fuck you," I try to say from behind his palm as I buck my hips in an attempt to throw him off. I'm not going by anyone's rules, especially some stalker who broke into my fucking house.

He tsks before moving around. I pause and squint my eyes as I try to decipher his movements.

Fuck, I think he's pulling something out of his pocket, but it's hard to tell with how dark it is.

I open my mouth wide, stretching it to its limit, and sink my teeth into his hand with a powerful bite.

He comes back down with his face centimeters from mine. "By all means, bite me harder. I love the pain," he says before licking the side of my neck and giving it a bite so hard that I'm sure it will leave a mark.

My mouth opens from the shock of the pain on a gasp. He takes the opportunity of my guard being down and removes his hand before shoving something in my mouth and flipping me over onto my stomach like a rag doll. I hear a click at the back of my head and still.

Holy fucking shit.

There's a gag in my mouth.

He grabs both of my wrists in iron grips and places them palm down by my head before anchoring himself above me. He then pushes my hands into the mattress while rubbing his very hard cock back and forth against my ass.

As he shifts back slightly, a groan rumbles deep in his throat, expressing his delight.

"Did you wear this with me in mind?" he asks, pulling on the black satin sleep dress I bought yesterday. "You wanted me to come through your window. You wanted me to see you in this, didn't you?"

I'm unsure what to say because, on some level, I pictured being touched like last night with this on. The buttery-soft material on the hanger gave me a zap of arousal right in my core. My thighs literally rubbed together in the middle of the boutique to ease some of my sexual tension.

He pulls the short dress up above my hips and groans again.

Shit.

"And no fucking panties. Was that meant for me, too? Hmm?"

I shake my head and moan as he drags his finger up and down my slit. Slowly. Teasingly. A featherlight touch.

I buck up against him, and I'm not sure if it's to get him off me or to have him apply more pressure.

"Such a good girl for everyone else to see, but such a bad little lamb for me." His voice is rough, but there's a hint of satisfaction in his words.

I can't help but let out a throaty moan as he continues with his torturous rhythm. Not giving me enough to push me over the edge of ecstasy but enough to push me to the edges of insanity.

"You're so wet for me right now. You're leaking out onto my fingers."

"Please," I groan against the gag.

"What was that?"

"Please," I repeat.

His warm breath is right against my ear. "You want to play nice now?" He thrusts against my ass. "What about when you left me on read, baby?" *Thrust.* "Was that playing nice?" *Thrust.* "I don't tolerate being ignored." *Thrust.* "I'm going to need more than a please." *Thrust.*

He's driving me insane.

The rough fabric of his pants rubs against my ass with every thrust, adding a sting of friction to my cold, exposed skin. I will literally say anything at this point to get him to make me come. The thought is worrisome, but that's how much he's turning me on.

"I didn't hear you, baby. What was that?" He laughs before changing our position.

His hard length pushes into my stomach as I'm face down, ass up in his lap.

My breathing becomes more erratic as warring unease and excitement surge through me.

"Looks like you need a lesson in what happens when you ignore me." He lifts my night dress back up to my hips before caressing the globe of my ass cheek. A light warmth covers my cheeks as I think about how exposed this position makes me. I'd be embarrassed if I wasn't so turned on. He rubs in a circle, first one cheek, then the other. The motion is soothing and encompasses me in a calmness.

"You'll count every strike. If you don't, we'll start again."

"Count?" I ask through the gag, completely confused.

I turn back to look at him. "Eyes forward," he says while grabbing ahold of the back of my neck and pushing me back down.

I take a couple of deep breaths, trying to calm my racing heart as I wait for something to happen.

I'm shocked when I experience a whack followed by immense pain on my right ass cheek that radiates to my core and burns so good.

He tsks three times at me. "Looks like we'll start again."

Fuck, I forgot to count.

"One, please, one," I shriek.

"Doesn't count."

How can he understand what I'm saying through this gag?

He runs the tip of his fingers on my skin, softly raising goose bumps in his wake and intensifying the burn.

He stops his caress and spanks me again. My body moves forward with the motion, and my eyes squeeze shut because of the pain and pleasure.

"One."

"Good girl," he whispers while rubbing my slit. His deep, praising voice creates a whirlwind of butterflies in my stomach, leaving me perplexed.

I always thought the *good girl* talk was cliché and overdone, but coming from him...

In quick succession, he spanks me four more times. Every one of those I count in hopes of hearing him call me a good girl again.

I would happily accept more to experience him saying those words again.

What the hell is he doing to me?

By the time I count to ten, I'm shaking.

Each smack is closer to my core and makes my clit throb in anticipation. If he would land just a little lower, I could cum. Though I think he knows that and doesn't on purpose.

"You like that, baby? You like your ass nice and red from my hand?" He starts his featherlight touches again, which brings forth more goose bumps. "Only I can touch you like this. No one else will ever touch you the way I do."

And then he smacks my center before inserting his thumb into my core and rubbing my clit with his other fingers. My eyes roll into the back of my head as my back arches. No one has ever touched me like this. It's heaven and hell, and I never want it to stop. I surrender to my senses. The way my core clenches around his digit with each thrust, the sweet burn taking over my body.

I'm drooling, and on the verge of an orgasm I'm unsure I'll ever come back from.

His expert strokes are rough and demanding.

My muted moans fill the room and accompany his heavy breathing.

"Be a good girl and come."

The second he murmurs those two words from his lips, I'm a goner.

My hips buck, and stars shoot behind my eyes as he relentlessly pumps his thumb into me until I can't take any more.

He kisses my side. "You're so beautiful when you come with my finger inside you."

He helps me off his lap and tucks me back into bed. I barely sense him taking the gag from my mouth and kissing my forehead before sleep claims me.

Nine

Gage

As I watch her drift into a satisfied sleep, I long to climb in behind her and feel the softness of her skin against mine, to entwine our bodies between the sheets of her bed.

A groan escapes my throat as I place my thumb in my mouth, indulging in her exquisite taste that still lingers. I've fantasized about what she gave me tonight for as long as I can remember. The combination of her obedience while counting through the ball gag, and the heat from my hand on her perfect ass sent a wave of exhilaration through me.

Despite her lack of understanding, her body longs for the embrace of submission. I sensed it the night at the club and felt it again tonight. There's an internal struggle within her mind, but only until she surrenders to the pleasure and relinquishes control.

Moving closer, I take the same thumb and run it along her pouty lips before rubbing away the rest of her tears. I'll only ever make her cry tears of unadulterated joy and ecstasy.

When I got out of prison, I observed her and noted how she had become a mere shadow of her former vibrant self. I noticed a difference in her demeanor—she seemed more reserved, not exuding the confident aura that I was familiar with her having.

I don't know when it started, but I know Marco was one of the reasons for the change in her. He treated her like shit when all she ever wanted was his love and acceptance. He threw it away like he's always done.

---

8 YEARS AGO

My brother Marco and I are in my father's office. As we've grown, we've been coming in here more and more lately for meetings, as my father likes to call them.

Most include unpleasant teaching methods that leave us with scars. Mentally and physically.

I hate the motherfucker I call my father. He's so formal and detached from his emotions. One day, I'm going to kill him. Mom will be upset. Which is the only reason I haven't tried it yet. I still don't understand what my mother sees in him. He's an intimidating man, well over six feet, with dark features, a god complex, and a sadistic mind.

We're learning about the family business and what our roles will be in the organization once we're of age in a few short years.

The future we have ahead of us will be very dark. A broad spectrum of very illegal and morally black activities we will not only take part in, but reign over. One that I will try to keep my sister, Ro, *away from. She's not meant for this life. She's meant for her happily ever after she always talks about with hearts in her eyes.*

"You can't be serious, Dad," Marco says with an upset huff.

"What gave you any indication I've ever been anything besides serious?"

"I don't want to marry her. I barely even like her."

My heated gaze swings to my brother like he's grown a second head. He's such a douche.

"I don't give a fuck whether you like her or not. It's your duty as a part of this family."

"Why does it have to be me? Why can't it be him?" My brother hikes his finger over at me.

"I'll do it," I say with a shrug, not giving away how on edge I am. Alexa isn't someone who should be discarded. She's special. Any man who ends up with her one day should be thrilled. She has an amazing personality, is pretty, and makes me laugh.

"Absolutely not. Your brother was the firstborn and will take the responsibility. You will be his right hand, and I will find you someone suitable to marry when the time comes."

"He was born three minutes before me. That's hardly considered the old—"

"I refuse to listen to this anymore. The decision is final." My father cuts me off and lays down the law. "Now leave and change your attitudes before I find a way to change them." With that, we're dismissed.

We make our way out of the office and up to the game room, which also houses a huge theater screen.

Laughter carries from down the hall, and I instantly make out Alexa's sweet little laugh. A lovely melody that always brings a smile to my face.

They're sitting on the overstuffed white couches and watching some comedy that has them rolling. Alexa's whole face lights up, and her eyes sparkle when she laughs. I can't help but watch her with awe.

Marco comes up to my side. "This whole thing blows. Why do I have to be the oldest?"

"This isn't a bad thing. You're lucky you're ending up with her. At least you've known her all your life. She won't be a stranger you have to marry," I say in a hushed tone. I don't want her to know any of this. It would upset her if she learned Marco's opinion of her.

"You should marry her then," Marco says with a bite in his tone.

"I tried. You heard our father," I say with displeasure.

I don't see what the big deal is. If we have to marry into her family, why can't it be me? My father's reasoning makes little sense, but nothing ever does with him. It's like he hates me and wants me to be miserable.

"You didn't try hard enough. You never do. I'll figure out a way to change this on my own. No way I'm letting this happen," he says with one last scathing look over at Alexa before walking out.

I swear I want to strangle him. He doesn't deserve to be a leader or have her. He's weak and lazy.

I make my way over to the girls and decide to sit closer to Alexa on purpose.

Like I always do.

We're about two feet apart, but the moment I sit down, I get that same feeling. The electricity that zaps between her and me.

The yearning to get closer to her, to touch her, keeps me on edge for the rest of the movie.

Rosie has since fallen asleep and is lightly snoring on the chaise lounge along the other side of the couch.

The credits are rolling, and the room is shrouded in darkness, besides the white from the lettering on the screen.

I take a chance and gaze over at her. She's looking straight ahead and seems to be in deep thought.

"Hey, Lex," I whisper and reach out to touch her arm. "You okay?"

"Yeah, I'm good," she says with a bright smile that makes my heart beat faster.

"I just made a new playlist. Do you want to listen with me?" I ask as I reluctantly remove my hand from her arm and grab my phone.

Alexa and I have the same taste in music, so I'm always making new playlists and saving them on my old iPod for her to listen to.

"Duh." She grabs the remote and presses mute before jumping back on the couch and closer to me. We're now sitting side by side, shoulders almost touching.

From her proximity, I can smell her sweet candy and coconut perfume I love so much. Last winter, I let her borrow my jacket one night when she was cold. When I got it back, it had this exact scent. I smelled it until her scent, unfortunately, faded away. That sounds creepy, but she makes me happy, and I love being in her presence.

Thoughts of her never go away. They play on repeat, just like my favorite songs.

I still don't know the moment I fell for her, but I did.

My crush is turning into something more powerful. Something that's sure to burn me alive and leave me in pain forever. She isn't mine to have, but I can't help but gravitate toward her.

Moments alone with her are rare, but when I get them, I cherish each second like it might be my last.

I hit the first song on my playlist, and the surround sound speakers pick it up at once. I watch her face as she hears the first song.

The song talks about finding your love while I'm busy looking at mine. Her head bobs to the music, making her hair shimmy around her shoulders. She's so cute, and she doesn't even try.

It reminds me of when I was watching her dance around in my mother's garden one night with Rosie. It was impossible to ignore, or perhaps I should say hear, considering they were screaming a song at the top of their lungs into the sky while dancing around in the rain. Perhaps that's when I first realized Lex was more than a friend.

She had a dark green dress that swayed in the wind as her hips moved. Her hair was longer back then and a little wild. Her fair skin looked so pretty under the moonlight, like an ethereal goddess.

Then, the dress started molding to her body from the rain, her hair sticking to her skin.

I remember wanting to be the rain droplets, covering her body completely with mine.

I register her staring right at me as a different song plays on the speakers.

When did the other song end?

A wave of regret washes over me. I should savor every second with her and not daydream.

"Whatcha looking at, silly?" she asks with a huge smile.

Your beautiful face.

"Nothing," I blurt before averting my eyes. I can't believe she caught me staring, and I didn't notice.

There goes the electricity popping between us again. I wonder if she can feel it too. I gaze back over, right into her big doe eyes.

I find myself mesmerized, unable to avert my gaze. The lyrics combined with her proximity are maddening.

With a slow, deliberate move, I inch my hand closer to hers until our fingers nearly touch. Her eyes stay trained on me, but I can see her chest heaving. She feels it too. She has to.

I decide to take the moment further, because if I don't, I'll probably die. I slowly move my hand on top of hers and thread our fingers together, rubbing the side of her pinky finger with my thumb.

Her skin under my hand is so soft, and fits in mine like it was made for my hand.

She inhales deeply as she looks down at our joined hands. The tension in the air is thick.

Her fingers squeeze mine before she gazes back up at me.

I've never been closer to her than right now. My heart is beating a mile a minute. I lean in closer to her, and she does the same. Our foreheads touch, and our lips are inches apart. I move my mouth closer to hers until our lips are touching, just barely. Like a secret whispered between lovers.

Someone flips the switch, bathing us in light.

We jerk apart like we're doing something wrong.

But why does it feel so right?

Alexa looks over at me with her fingers on her lips, and her eyes heated in a way I've never seen.

"What's going on, guys? Why're you in the dark?" I glare at Marco, conveying my annoyance.

The wrong twin is going to end up with the treasure.

Ten

Alexa

The following morning, I wake up with aches in my muscles as I stretch. I open my eyes and sit up with a jolt.

Last night hammers into my brain with every devious memory on repeat. My eyes go straight to the slider, which now sits closed.

Was it a dream? Because if so, wow.

This has been by far one of the most eventful weekends I've had since leaving college, which was an impulse decision, but one I have yet to regret. Although my dad was hesitant about my choice to leave, he understood my reasons, which tipped the scales and made it easier.

I'm sure my mom influenced his decision. They've always been inseparable, and my dad has yet to tell her no. I fell under the same category the second I was born. My dad can be scary and a true hard-ass, but he's always treated my mom and me like queens. Perhaps it's due to my status as an only child and his being surrounded by girls. Two to one. He never stood a chance.

Still, I made a deal with him. I'd continue to accompany him to meetings to learn the ins and outs of the business and keep up with the books. A job I was given after finding discrepancies in the ledgers my dad's accountant allegedly missed when I was sixteen. I'll never forget that day in his office. I was going through the spreadsheets to familiarize myself with the companies we own and where our money goes when I realized the math wasn't adding up. I checked it four times before I informed my dad, and within three hours, I witnessed the gruesome scene as my dad mercilessly tortured and killed his long-standing accountant, who had embezzled over five hundred thousand dollars from our businesses throughout the years. Though it was a rough day, it was also one of the best I've had since the fateful night I was almost killed. It was the first time I felt a glimmer of my worth to the organization, and the look of pride and respect on my dad's face was everything I had hoped to have. It was like a craving, and I strive to continue to make him proud.

That leads to my next issue. The impending arranged marriage, or rather, lack thereof. My future was always set in stone, and I accepted my fate a long time ago. I knew I would take my dad's place, and an arranged marriage was mandatory. Now, I have no clue what will happen, or who I will have to marry. Although Dad said it will be a cold day in hell before I marry Marco after he cheated on me.

It's baffling how time shows you someone's true colors. I built Marco up so high in my head after the kiss in college. It felt like a pressure lifted off my shoulders. I believed him to be everything I ever wanted and someone I could be happy with.

But as I look back, it's almost like a stranger looking into someone else's life. There were signs I'd missed while wearing my rose-colored glasses, such as the less-than-thrilled expressions he sent my way over the years, or the subtle ways he showed me he wasn't interested.

When I learned he was my intended, my dad told me he had known for quite some time. I can reflect now and find moments of Marco's almost hatred toward the idea of it or, rather, of me. Probably both. From me being cold and him refusing to give me his jacket, only for Gage to give me his, to him dismissing me on the night of the dance, I now consider a black night. The night Gage was ripped away and never said goodbye.

Many times, I've wondered what it would have been like to end up with Gage. If he would have never gone away, if he would have been mine.

As I matured, the way I felt about him altered, and my childhood adoration gave way to more complex feelings. He was my best friend in so many ways, but often someone I would think about at night. His touches appeared more intimate to me, his hugs longer than usual, and his looks would set me ablaze from the inside out.

I would always hold his burning gaze like a war for who would avert their eyes first, and the gazes always lasted a little too long for just friends. It started small. First, it was recognizing how good he smelled, then it was the contoured lines of his Apollo's belt that led to his swim trunks. It was then I realized it was transforming into something more.

I never said anything because I was worried it would ruin our closeness.

Then the game room incident happened. I remember noticing every time he looked my way. It was just us in the dark, listening to a new playlist he made for me. The lyrics hit differently than they ever had.

The selection of songs was for a lover, not a friend.

I felt his hand move closer to mine. The time it took was agonizing. He wasn't even touching me, but I could still feel him. Once his hand rested on mine and rubbed, I got a strange sensation in my core I can now deduct as arousal.

The moment our foreheads touched, I felt like I was one with him, imagining all these different scenarios of what we could be.

I let the feelings blossom in my chest, knowing he felt something for me, too.

The barely there kiss set my world on fire.

Only for the lights to be flipped on and reality to set in. A couple of days later, I was told I'd be marrying Marco.

From that day forward, I shoved all thoughts of Gage from my mind because it wasn't right, and it wasn't fair to his brother. I threw him back into the friend's-only category, and it's where he stayed.

And I suppose that's where he will always remain, especially after learning he's returned but lacks the desire to find me.

I fall back onto my pillow, too lazy to get up, only to hear something bump against my headboard. I glance upward and noticed a necklace with an Atocha Emerald at its end. Quickly, I jump up to retrieve it.

This necklace isn't mine, but the resemblance to the one I lost in college is remarkable. I was so devastated when I couldn't find it. It was a birthday present from my Nonna before she passed away. She was very much into stones; it was the last gift she ever gave me.

I still remember her saying the emerald is known as the stone of successful love. Not in my case, unfortunately.

My fingers run over the grooves and ridges I can almost swear were on the one I lost.

As I take it off the poster of my bed, I see a small tag toward the clasp engraved with a date: 11.25.23. How odd. I inspect it, but the date isn't ringing a bell, especially since it's dated not too far into the future. A little less than two months or so.

I shrug and put it on anyway before grabbing my phone. Messages galore greet me.

Unknown

> I see you've found my gift. A token of appreciation for how you came on my fingers so sweetly last night.

The color drains from my face. It wasn't a dream.

I check the sliding glass door that's locked before heading to the front, which is also locked.

Alexa

> How the hell did you get in?

Unknown

> No thank you? I have to say, your manners are terrible. First, a free dinner, and now a necklace with no appreciation? You're going to hurt my feelings, baby.

He paid for the dinner I had with Jenna... I should have known. I'm such an idiot.

A sharp pain blossoms behind my eyes, the prelude to a migraine, and I press my fingers to my temples, attempting to soothe the agonizing pulse. All thanks to this faceless, nameless stranger whose presence is both comforting and unsettling. I ought to be ashamed for allowing a stranger to touch me repeatedly, as this is unlike my typical behavior, but I'm not. I preserved my purity for a man who deceived me and was unfaithful. While I'm not actively seeking more, the absence of the arranged marriage makes it easier to let go and see what happens.

Jenna would be pleased with the turn of events, but I don't dare tell her. I would never hear the end of it.

Alexa

> The restraining order is happening.

Unknown

> We've already been over this, baby. You didn't seem too upset last night.

This fucking guy. I'm at a loss for words because I truly enjoyed last night. There must be something wrong with me.

I try a new tactic.

Alexa

> Why me? I'm sure there are many girls at your disposal to stalk and bother.

Unknown

> None of them holds any value to me besides you.

Alexa

> I'm a possession to you?

Unknown

> You're everything to me. I couldn't categorize you as just one thing.

Okay, not what I expected him to say, considering his usual crude words and sexual innuendos.

Uknown

> **Have dinner with me on Wednesday night.**

Alexa

> **No.**

Unknown

> **Okay, so I'll come back into your house tonight. Say, when you're asleep again, then start where I left things. That sounds much better than eating, anyway... Well, I guess I'll still be eating, and you will be too when I shove my cock down your throat and make you drink my cum.**

My eyes bulge out of my head as a tingle finds its way into my stomach. Holy fucking shit. I'm so out of my league here.

Alexa

> **Fine, where and when?**

Unknown

> **I knew you'd come around, baby. My driver will pick you up at six.**

Alexa

> ***middle finger emoji**

Unknown

> **Oh, piccolo angello, your wish is my command. I've been dreaming about plunging into your depths for a lifetime.**

Unknown

> **But... I'm going to need you to beg.**

Alexa

> **NOT A CHANCE IN HELL**

Eleven

Gage

Something about her feisty temper brings a smile to my face. This is a side to her I briefly got to enjoy before I left. I love her sweet and caring side, but this one brings forth entirely different feelings. Deviant ones I can't wait to explore with her.

I watch her walk through her little place on my computer screens, throwing up middle fingers in every direction. If I was smart, I wouldn't have given myself away, but fuck, I couldn't help myself. I wanted to see her face when she put two and two together about me watching her. She didn't disappoint.

I'm not trying to be a stalker per se, well, fuck, a little, but it's also for her protection.

She strolls into the bathroom, and I decide to get back to work. I may be a fucking creep, but I won't invade her privacy in that way.

I get back into my paperwork, which seems to be never-ending. My fingers are in too many cookie jars and I can't seem to give myself a break. It's like swimming through different currents of water all moving around at once. Pulling me in every direction, I'm just trying to make sure I don't drown.

It's been this way since I got out. I gave my father a big fuck you and started my own businesses while using connections I made while in prison. They were well aware of my identity and the unique skills I could contribute, and I was equally aware of how I could leverage their abilities. Before I even left, countless partnerships were established. Bit by bit, I've been unraveling the empire my father holds so dear. Soon enough, everything that once existed will disappear, and my father's name will lose its power, reduced to only a faint murmur.

It's strange how violence can either bring you together or force you apart. My father was the latter. He made me hate him to an unimaginable level. If there's something further than hatred, that's what I hold for him. It took a long time to sift through all the tangled emotions and ingrained beliefs he made me carry. So many scars he inflicted, and for what? I still rose from the ashes where he left me, and I'm better than ever. My best friend, Vic, was the former. He had my back in prison. If not for him, I wouldn't have survived the second time I was attacked. Blood doesn't mean shit. Sometimes it's just an excuse. Sometimes you need to bleed out that blood and become anew.

A knock makes me look up to see Jace. *He's another one where I could say violence brought us together,* I think with a grin.

The week following my prison release, I was lost in the television's glow while in Vic's living room when I heard a noise and checked out the blinds. Someone was rooting around the front porch at one in the morning. After their third failed attempt at getting through a window, I unlocked the back door and waited for them to come around. I wanted the guy to get in just as badly as he apparently wanted to get in. I thought it was one of my father's men coming for me. As he walked in through the back and made his way into the kitchen, I jumped him from behind and wrestled him to the ground. His fight was laughable, to say the least, and once he said Vic's name, I let him go and turned on the light.

A guy younger than me was looking back at me with a black eye and a busted lip. I was rough but didn't throw my hands. Turns out, he was Axl, Vic's friend's little cousin. Vic allowed Jace to flop at his house when he got into fights with his old man. Once he told me, my heart squeezed. I found a kinship with him at that moment. From that day forward, he's been like a little brother I never asked for but got anyway.

It felt good to pay it forward and be the guiding light he needed, mirroring Vic's support when I first became his cellmate. I made him a deal and gave him a safe place to stay a week after we met. Now, he handles every errand for the club, and any other inconveniences I don't have time for.

"What's up?"

"Just checking in. I didn't get the chance to talk the other night."

"No worries. I got a piece of what I needed. What happened, though? Your charms didn't work on the friend?"

"My charms work on everybody," he says with a smile so big both of his dimples show. "Some guy came up to her at the bar, whispered something in her ear, and she went white as a ghost. Then she ran to you guys."

"An ex or something?"

"No clue. It was fucking weird, though."

"Check the database and see who he is."

I won't tolerate someone harassing her friend, especially if it could endanger Alexa's safety as well. They seem to be together more often than not.

"On it," Jace says as he walks out of my office while typing something into his phone.

My phone rings, and I get a call from the front. I have a visitor. A very unwelcome visitor. I count to ten and hope that, for his sake, I have enough patience to deal with him.

I raise my eyes just as my carbon copy waltzes in. His hair looks picture-perfect, and he's dressed like he just had brunch at a country club before a golf tournament.

Where I went dark with tattoos and muscle on muscle, he went light with a clean-cut fuckboy appearance and a runner's body. A body I'm sure would be easy to bend in half and break.

Our contrasting appearances are impossible to ignore, more pronounced than ever before, which makes a calmness wash over me.

I got locked up because of this motherfucker. Years wasted, never to be replaced.

If we weren't twins, identical ones at that, I would have never had to pay a price with years of my life. His penance is coming, and I look forward to it.

I spent many years thinking of creative and imaginative ways I would make him pay. Some more painful than others. The weirdest revelation is my choice to wait out his punishment.

When I got locked up, an overwhelming anger surged through me, fueling my every thought and action. The darkness was so overwhelming, all I could see was a pitch-black void. It consumed my every thought. I was fortunate to have Vic teach me how to turn my anger into a source of strength to push forward.

Instead of self-destruction, I used my time to better myself. I gained weight and muscle, read thousands of books, finished my schooling, and started college business courses.

I went through a metamorphosis in my time behind bars. I was no longer the good twin who ripped the shirt off his back, no matter how badly I needed it for myself.

I no longer sacrificed my own needs to appease others.

I pledged my loyalty solely to myself and to those who would reciprocate my every action.

I keep my circle small. Until proven otherwise, I perceive everyone as a potential adversary and that includes so-called blood.

That's what makes this motherfucker in front of me an unwelcome presence. He's the enemy. I understand my father manipulated events and used me as a scapegoat, but Marco's choices caused all subsequent events.

"To what do I owe this unfortunate visit, Marco?" I murmur from behind my desk.

I don't get up and do the brotherly hug shit or extend an arm out for him to sit. And I sure as fuck don't gaze back up at his stupid ass when there are more pressing matters to attend to.

"Come on, don't be like that, little bro. I've missed you," he says, scanning his surroundings from what I can see in my periphery. "You got a nice place here. Definitely an interesting choice in a business venture, if I do say so myself."

"Is there a reason you're here?" I say, peering up at him. He's now sitting on my black leather couch off to the right. His feet are propped up on my glass table like he has every right to sit there, with no care in the world. "Don't you have an empire to run?"

"You're supposed to help me run the family business as my right hand, remember?"

"I'm no one's fucking lapdog, and I don't work for anyone besides myself."

"You can be my partner." Hope fills his eyes. What a fool.

"You think I want to be anywhere near your stupid ass? Even seeing you right now makes me want to stab you in the fucking neck."

"No reason to get all prison inmate on me. I'm here to offer you what you've always wanted."

The comment makes my jaw tick, my fists clench, and a burning rage threatens to consume me, yet I refuse to give in to violence. "And what do you think I've always wanted?"

"Easy. Alexa... and the empire you're trying so hard to stay away from and dismantle."

The mention of her name piques my interest. However, I maintain a bored demeanor.

"What makes you think I want either of those?"

He laughs. "You must think I'm stupid, Gage. You've been in love with her since we were kids." Despite my racing heart, I maintain a stoic expression as he persists, "All those stolen glances resembling a lovesick puppy."

I steeple my hands against my chin, my eyes narrowing with an intense glare. "Do you intend to waste my entire day with your pointless chatter, or are you going to make your point?"

"My point is, I'll give you what you've always wanted. The family business and the girl."

"And how do you suppose you'll do that? From what I hear, Alexa is no longer yours."

"I did that for you. Everything over the past few years has been for you," he says quickly. "It's the least I can do after you went to prison for me."

He finally said it. What I've been waiting years to hear. This motherfucker never even apologized when I got taken in. He hid in his room like a little bitch.

16 YEARS OLD

"Here they come," Mom says, rushing in with a camera.

My gaze rises as Rosie and Alexa descend the stairs.

Mom gives me a kiss on the way to the girls. "Thank you for taking them shopping today, honey."

"Of course," I say, but barely register anything else besides Alexa.

She looks beautiful. A light smoky eye and red lips. She opted for a black strapless dress with jewels covering the tulle bottom, making the light catch the dress and sparkle just like her eyes.

I feel a dark presence at my side just as Marco steps up next to me. He's been in a shitty mood for months. We haven't been able to stand each other, and from the smell, he's been drinking again. If our father finds out, there will be hell to pay. He's already fixed multiple fuckups of his that were alcohol-induced.

Alexa looks over and sees him. "What do you think, Marco?" She does a twirl.

"About what?" he says before walking away.

What a fucking piece of shit. I almost go to follow him until I see Alexa's face fall.

"When am I going to get a picture with you guys?" I say, hoping to shift the expression on Alexa's face.

I walk between my sister and Alexa. "You look beautiful, Lex," I whisper in Alexa's ear before looking forward and smiling into the lens.

We've never mentioned the moment we shared in the game room that night a year ago.

It will always be a core memory for me, something I've re-played many times.

The moment she found out about her arranged marriage to Marco, our relationship underwent a shift. It was like a dagger to my heart. I had no hope.

"Are you girls ready to go? The limo's here," Mom says with a wide smile.

Mom's always gone against my father to make sure Rosie got all the experiences she never had, including the homecoming dance the girls are going to tonight. One Marco and I could have gone to if my father hadn't forbidden it.

The girls walk by and I give them one last hug before they're off.

As we sit down to dinner later that night, my father gets a call.

One that would change the course of my life forever.

Someone died in a car crash, a hit and run, to be more exact.

Witnesses saw the driver, and it was someone who looked just like me, but wasn't me.

Within the next hour, I turn myself in for a crime I never committed.

My brother is due to reign over the kingdom my father has kept alive for decades.

Marco had already fucked up too much, and this couldn't be swept under the rug with bribes and money. Something the families have used to their advantage for decades.

Someone had to pay for the crime.

I was the expendable second-born son.

Never did I hate my brother or father more than the moment the bars clicked closed in my cell.

I was never the same after that day.

The devil in me was summoned forth to lead in my vendetta.

A new monster was born, which rivaled the one I always kept locked away.

Present

"How did you suppose treating her like shit would bring her my way?"

"Isn't she already in your territory?" he asks knowingly before he grins.

The fucker's been watching us. Although I'm certain he's only been to my club today. I have cameras all over the place. His sniffing around and watching her unsettles me. I'll have to check her place the next time I sneak in and make sure my cameras are the only ones in residence.

"All you're showing is that you're a stalker bitch."

"A stalker bitch who's trying to make things right." He grins.

I don't like his grin; it puts me on edge.

"And why don't you want the empire you've been groomed to take over?"

"You know I've never wanted it. I just went with it to get the old man off my case. I'm not meant to lead."

"And what makes you think I am?" I ask with a raised brow.

"Come on, baby bro, you're smart, lethal, determined, and you've always wanted it. The empire and the girl. What do you say?"

"I'll think about it," I say to get him out of my office and, more importantly, out of my fucking face.

Twelve

Alexa

As requested, or more like forced, I'm ready ten minutes prior to when the driver will arrive.

I went back and forth with myself on whether to tell him to fuck off or just go with it. I went with the latter, telling myself I'd get free food out of it.

What? A girl has to eat.

I also find something weird about him I can't quite put my finger on. So I'm curious, just like the night at the club that started all of this. My curiosity will get me killed one day.

Rosie and I have always been notorious for going places we shouldn't to get the scoop. Well, more so me, but I'd always drag her along.

It was like a treasure hunt, and the answers at the end were the prize. I used to get in so much trouble. My nose was always where it didn't belong. I can't help but smile at the thought of how mischievous I was as a kid.

A text notification from who I now have labeled as "Stalker" comes through, telling me the car is outside.

I make my way out to the blacked-out Cadillac Escalade, where the door is already open and waiting. I stop for a moment. This would be the time to go back if I had any self-preservation left in me.

My phone beeps again, and I know exactly who it is. I roll my eyes and say fuck it before climbing in. The door shuts, and I'm bathed in darkness, aside from the starlight headliner above. The partition is up, so I assume it will be a quiet ride to wherever we're going. I decide to use this moment to check my phone.

Stalker

> Get in the damn car.

I can't help but laugh. I'm sure my stubbornness is driving him mad.

Stalker

> Don't start that, baby. You'll get yourself eaten before you even have time to eat dessert.

The tension in my body intensifies as his dirty words stir up a deep ache, prompting a desperate need for release. The black leather seats do little to soothe my flushed skin and the prickling sensation in my core.

Stalker

> You like when I talk to you like this, don't you? I can see you rubbing your legs together. Trying to satisfy the ache. Just know, not you nor anyone else will ever be able to make you feel as good as I do.

"You have cameras in here?" I murmur to no one in particular as I'm all by myself. My phone beeps, and I direct my gaze downward.

Stalker

> Of course I do. I like to look at you.

"You're absolutely insane. Ever heard of a little thing called privacy?" I say aloud.

My eyes scan the partition, air vents, and the roof of the car. I'm sure that ass is laughing at me right now. I decide to give him the universal sign of fuck you with both of my middle fingers.

Stalker

> There's no such thing as privacy when it comes to you.

"Why?"

Stalker

> I want all of you, not just pieces.

I read that sentence for what feels like a million times with my mouth shut.

I get jolted out of my inner musings to see that we've stopped. The moment I step out, I realize we're at the club that started this whole fiasco. I go to take a step back toward the car as a guy comes walking up to me. He's familiar for some reason.

"Hey, I'm Jace. I'll bring you inside." From the voice, I can tell it's definitely not him. This guy has buzzed blond hair and a beard that's grown out a couple of weeks. He's cute with the dimples, but I like my guys a little darker in appearance. I think this is the guy Jenna danced with that night.

As I walk beside him, I can't help but notice that we're taking a different entrance than the one I used the first time. The complete absence of noise in this room is almost eerie and puts me on edge as my heels click against the floor.

"Why's it so vacant tonight? Last time I was here, it was pretty packed."

"The boss closed the club for you to eat dinner," he says while continuing his pace through a zigzag of rooms and hallways. Everything is still just as magical and dreamy as the last time.

My steps falter. "Wait... He owns this place?"

My throat almost closes at the thought, and I try to swallow the lump down. This should change everything... shouldn't it? I can't keep up with someone like this. I already felt like I was out of my element, but now I'm way beyond that.

"Yep." He stops in front of a black door with intricate carvings and gold hardware. Over the door is a sign that says Four Senses.

How odd. This place is like falling down the hole in *Alice in Wonderland*.

"If you will," he extends his arm, and I examine it in question. "You're going to use my arm for a minute, if that's okay?"

"Why?" The second the word is out of my mouth, my phone beeps. Rolling my eyes, I grab his arm.

"Your boss is a pain in the ass."

"Don't I know it." He laughs as we walk into complete darkness.

The second the door closes, another set of arms are grabbing me.

"I've missed you," a voice says with lips so close to my ear it gives me goose bumps.

"How can you see me in the dark? And why are we in the dark?"

"We'll dine in complete darkness. It'll give you the chance to use your other senses while your sight is taken away. I promise you the food will taste and smell better, your hearing will be more attuned to the sounds around you, and my touches will feel even better."

Okay, not what I expected at all. This is a first. I did not know things like this existed.

"And how are you able to see?"

"I have night vision goggles on, of course."

"Why do you get to see, and I don't?"

"Because I'm going to feed you."

He leads me to a table and helps me sit. It's awkward as hell not being able to see. It also takes a tremendous level of trust I don't think I've ever given to a practical stranger.

As I was getting ready earlier, I grabbed the holster for my knife but stopped and opted to go without it. Something in my gut told me I didn't need it. He may want me for deviant activities, but I don't think he would put me in danger or hurt me.

"You look beautiful tonight. The red dress is a pleasant touch. It'll look great on my floor later."

"He's a cocky one...how charming."

"I prefer to call it confidence. Are you ready to eat?"

"What are we having?"

"Mediterranean food."

The unmistakable sound of a door being pushed open fills the room. I turn my head toward the noise, even though I can't see anything.

"My favorite," I smile. The aroma of fresh and earthy notes hit me the second it lands on the table, making my mouth water.

I feel a hand touch my knee, and I squeal. "It's just me. I came closer to feed you." His hand lingers, running up to my thigh before stopping. "Open."

I comply, wrapping my mouth around a forkful. I moan as the rich flavors of lemon and garlic hit my tastebuds, only for him to chuckle in return.

The food is phenomenal.

"You seem to guess all my favorite things."

"Is that a bad thing?"

"It's a suspicious thing," I say around another bite of food.

"I won't hurt you, baby."

"Then what's with the secretiveness? I still haven't seen you. Hell, I don't even know your name."

"Isn't that part of the fun?"

"Not if I don't know what to call you."

"There are many things you can call me, baby," he says while rubbing a finger between the small gap in my thighs and hitting my clit with every swipe.

I'm at his mercy. Completely blind, yet acutely aware of all sensations. The light touch is so much stronger and more intense in the dark.

His firm hands separate my thighs, bringing my dress up just before my hips, making the cold air hit the inside of my legs.

I try to tug my dress down, but he grips my hands in his. "Place your palms on the chair's armrests. Don't move them. Good. Now open your mouth." His voice has a deep, raspy quality to it, and it makes me comply and melt at the same time.

I almost choke on my bite of chicken as his fingers rub across my lacy panties that are wet against my folds. His finger hooks into my panties before he pulls them to the side.

With my heart pounding and my grip on the chair tightening, I anxiously await his next move, my breath held in anticipation.

A cold object is placed on my knee, causing me to flinch. "Easy, it's just ice."

He runs the piece of ice up my leg before placing it over my slit. "Oh God!" I moan.

"That's one of the names you may call me."

Another piece of ice runs over my other leg. It stings before turning cold and soothing my hot, sensitive skin. The ice melts and drips down my thighs in an almost tickling sensation. But when he puts it on my clit, a zing of electricity runs through my core.

The suspense of the unknown is making me crazy. I bump my hips into his fingers that are holding the ice against me.

"Are you feeling needy?" he asks near my ear. "You want to come?"

"Yes," I say in a whisper.

"Yes, what? You know what you need to do."

My hesitation lasts only a second before I surrender to my needs and beg, just like he wanted me to do.

"Please make me come."

"As you wish," he rasps.

The sound of a chair scrapes the floor in front of me as his hands push my legs further apart. "Open your legs wider for me, baby."

I do as he commands. A clinking of ice sounds in a glass, and then his mouth is on me.

"Fuck," I cry out. The sensation of his mouth on my sensitive flesh is a peculiar mix of burning heat and chilling coldness that collides into euphoria.

As he licks my core, I grind my hips against his eager mouth. His arms wrap around my thighs as he opens my legs even more to feast on me.

I ride his face with long strokes before I scream out my release. My body tingles as the delicious aftershocks of pleasure pulse through me.

He groans. "You taste so fucking good."

"That was amazing," I say breathlessly, sounding cheesy as fuck but not caring in the slightest.

He runs his thumb and fingers against my jaw before leaning in and giving me a small kiss on my forehead. "You're perfect. Let me pull your dress down so we can have dessert."

"I thought you just had dessert."

He gives a throaty laugh. "You're my favorite kind of dessert, but this is for you. Open."

He places something in my mouth that smells like chocolate. This is going to go down as one of the best nights ever.

I wrap my lips around his fingers, and he groans. The chocolate is velvety smooth, and the ganache melts in my mouth. My mouth is watering the second I swallow the godly dessert.

"Is this chocolate entremet?" I ask in shock, as it's one of my favorite desserts of all time.

"You like it, baby?"

"It's delicious."

He feeds me a couple more bites, and I give a little yawn. Satiated from both the orgasm and the meal.

Strong arms grip under my knees and around my back, effortlessly picking me up and holding me against his hard chest. We walk through the dark room and out of a door that is equally dark on the other side.

"Where are you taking me?"

"Home."

"Why don't you ever ask for anything in return?" I thought that was the way things went. Especially in a situation like this. Whatever this is...

"I want many things, but I'm content with what I'm given... for now," he says as he holds me closer and inhales the scent of my hair.

I'm not sure what he feels like he's getting when I'm not reciprocating, but I let it be. Too exhausted for the back and forth.

My fingers run along the stone of the necklace that rests between my cleavage.

"You gave me this necklace."

"I did..."

"Why exactly?"

"You don't like it?" he asks with a hint of uncertainty.

"No, I love it. It's just... unique."

"As are you."

Whether I want them to or not, those words have a way of filling my heart with a special type of joy. It makes me feel cherished.

"But what about the date on the tag?"

He falls silent for a moment, and I long to catch a glimpse of his expression.

"Nothing you need to worry about right now."

Why all the hush-hush cloak-and-dagger secrecy; is something fishy going on?

"Has anyone ever told you how cryptic you are?"

I don't know how, but I sense his smile.

"Maybe a time or two."

Thirteen

Gage

"How'd the delivery go last night?" I ask as I turn to Vinny, my trusted enforcer and right-hand man, seated across from me at my desk in Obsidian.

As he stifles a yawn, he adjusts his posture, causing his shoulder-length black hair to brush against the top of his black suit jacket. I'm sure he's exhausted after spending the entire night organizing everything and having to deal with the complexities of playing both sides. Despite his long-standing employment with my father, he also carries out tasks for me. Giving me all the intel I need to take my father down.

"Decent. The crates were full of AKs, Baretta's, and revolvers. I took them to the McCormick warehouse."

"I want them to be distributed evenly between that warehouse, the one on Westside, and the one on Industrial. Get inventory of everything so I can start making some moves." I don't like the idea of that much money sitting in one place, even if guards are watching it.

"Done." The sound of paper crinkling reaches my ears as he hands me a list. I glance over at it and whistle. We stand to make a little over half a million from this stolen shipment, which belonged to my father. Though not significant by our standards, the money slowly undermines my father's way of living. The thought brings a smirk to my face.

"Perfect. Does my father suspect me?"

He shakes his head. "Hector suspects the Bratva. He backed out of a deal he made with Alexander Petrov for port access, and now they're at odds."

I gaze over at Vinny with a frown. "Why would he back out? They've been working together for decades."

"No clue. He's been making changes to the organization. Getting more suspicious and keeping things closer to the vest in the past few months."

I nod. "Makes sense with how everything is unraveling from beneath him."

"Because of the compromised location, he's receiving his next shipment of blow through the port in New York."

I want that shipment and any others bound for my father's hands. "Get ahold of Luciano for me. Tell him I want to meet. At this point, I'll pay him triple whatever my father does to use his port."

Vinny cringes.

"What?"

"Your father promised Luciano your sister's hand when she's found. That was the trade they made for him to use the port since Manuel called off the engagement when your sister ran."

"And why the hell am I just hearing about this now?"

Vinny shrugs as if this isn't a big deal. It is. I don't want anything happening to my sister. "I just found out, and I didn't think it would be an issue since you have her hiding in Indiana."

"No way am I offering my sister up to Luciano. The fucker is in his mid-fifties by now. Money will have to do. I don't care what it costs."

"And the Russians?" he asks as he twirls his ever-present knife between his fingers.

"It would be foolish of me to ignore this opportunity, a chance to benefit from their conflict. It's finally dawned on me why Alexander keeps asking for a meeting. He needs the relationship he's always had with the Chicago Mafia. It has the potential to unlock a lot of doors for us too, but the thought of a partnership makes me uneasy. There's a reason my father's relationship with the Russians has spanned decades."

"Alexander probably sees a change in the tides, with your father's reign falling and yours soaring."

"I guess there's only one way to find out," I say, reviewing my new inventory. "Call a few of the men and get everything moved no later than midnight tonight."

"I'll do that, then get some sleep. I'm fucking tired."

Vinny sits silently while fucking with his knife.

"Anything else?" I ask.

"What's going on with you and Alexa?"

"Why?" I furrow my brow.

"I saw her on the monitors the other night."

"She's mine."

"And what about her and Marco? Any chance you'll make them marry?"

At the mention of my brother, my hands ball into fists, the paper crackling under the pressure. "No. She's mine."

Vinny nods.

"Why do you care?" I ask with a tilt of my head.

Vinny shrugs as he stands and heads to the door. "Just want to make sure my cousin is with someone decent."

Once he's gone, my monitor flickers to life, showing Alexa sprawled on her couch, eyes crinkled with amusement as she laughs. From my distant vantage point, the sound still brings a comforting wave of warmth, a low hum that vibrates through the speakers and settles deep in my chest.

Decent is a foreign word in our world, but Vinny has nothing to worry about. I will treat Alexa with the utmost care and reverence.

"I don't know why we had to come all the way out here. There are a million places I'd rather be than this. Fucking Russia," Vinny spits as he shakes his head and rubs his hands together to keep warm.

I still don't have a clue what Vinny's so bent about. Chicago, although different, is also cold.

Ask him to torture someone within an inch of their life, filet their skin from their bones, and he's giddy. Ask him to take a little trip across the sea, and now he's all moody.

"You've been complaining nonstop since we left," I say, my words forming puffs of mist in the chilly air. "And you didn't seem to mind when we discussed this in my office two days ago."

"Lack of sleep had me tired. I don't trust the Bratva. History has taught us that."

"Sometimes it's time to change that history. More money, more reach, more power."

I gaze across the vast expanse of the snow-covered field. The relentless weather has shown no signs of easing since our arrival two hours ago. It's not uncommon for snow to be ten inches deep in early October, but it's been inconvenient as hell. Despite having a private plane, we still experienced delays due to the weather. My eyes go to my phone. It's six in the morning back in Chicago. As much as I longed to stay near Alexa, this business meeting couldn't be ignored. I skim our message thread and smirk. She gives as good as she gets.

An unanswered message sits in wait from Luciano. He was agreeable but was adamant that Rosie be part of that deal. Though he admitted he wants to marry her off to his son, who's in his early thirties, I don't like the idea of using my sister as a bargaining chip. She's not expendable. However, I'm torn. I know she'd be protected once she married into the New York outfit.

The sound of tires crunching on gravel reaches our ears as a black Aurus Senat pulls up outside the open hangar where we're seated.

Alexander steps out, looking far older than his thirty-eight years. The harsh cold has visibly aged him, yet it's apparent his unforgiving lifestyle has also played a part in his weathered appearance. Deep scars and wrinkles mar his face. His immense size and merciless behavior earned him the name The Brown Bear. Following his father's death eleven years ago, he took charge and has expanded his sphere of influence all the way into the US.

I rise from my seat, my footsteps echoing as I move toward him, bridging the gap between us as we meet halfway. His brown gloved hand reaches out to mine, and I take it while stabilizing myself. A man's handshake can reveal an abundance of details about his personality and character. With a forceful grip, he pulls me into his embrace, but I stand my ground, anticipating his actions, and squeeze his hand just as tightly while pulling him toward me. A smirk reaches his lips as he nods his head.

"I didn't know if you'd come, Moretti," Alexander says with his deep accent.

"Your invitations have been relentless."

"But they finally worked." He smirks.

"You said you wanted a meeting. Let's talk," I say, extending my arm back to the table and chairs where Vinny sits.

"All business, I see." He nods before sitting down and looking back at me. "My reach is growing, but so is yours. I have watched you acquire many territories and ports I had my eye on. Your father recently rescinded an agreement. I'm hoping to make a deal with you."

"You aren't taking over my territories or ports—" I say firmly and without hesitation. While I recognize the threat of his power and his reach, I won't let him intimidate me. I've fought relentlessly for years to reach this point, and I refuse to let anyone rip away my hard-earned accomplishments.

He laughs as he sparks up a cigarette and inhales deeply. "Is he always this serious?" Alexander questions Vinny, who ignores him with a slight expression of contempt.

Alexander gazes back over at me. "I'm looking for more of a partnership."

"I'm listening."

"I will give you access to the ports I have and a percentage of the guns and drugs if I can have access to your ports."

"What's the catch?"

He laughs. "You Italians, always so serious. I would like to arrange a marriage to unite us."

If he didn't say it so seriously, I'd probably laugh because there's no fucking way I'd unite us in that way.

"Isn't Roman a little young to be married off?" I ask, referring to his half brother, who's closer to my age than his.

His nose scrunches up, and he scoffs. "Roman still has his head up his ass in university. I'm talking about me. It's time I settled down and made a family. I need a legitimate heir."

The thought of him starting a family is unsettling. I've heard the whispers of the things they do in their secret society.

"I don't believe an arranged marriage would work for me."

"Why is that?"

"I don't want to be the reason for an innocent child to die."

He's quiet as he contemplates my words.

We might have our rules in the Mafia, but the secret society portion of the Bratva, The Void, is deplorable. If their firstborn is a girl, they kill her immediately. They see a firstborn female as weak and a stain on the family's name. A female can only be born after the son, their heir, is born. No fucking way am I going to be involved in something like that. The Mafia would have killed Alexa if we had done things like that, and that thought disgusts me.

"Your father said your sister would be available before we severed ties."

My skin crawls as my anger rises to the surface, and I'm tempted to kill my father the second I get back to the US. If I wasn't so dead set on sticking to my plan, I would. He dangled Rosie in front of everyone like a piece of meat to see who would benefit him the most. It's disgusting, and I'm tempted to speed up my plans so I can eliminate him sooner.

I shake my head. "My sister is already arranged to marry someone else."

Vinny glances at me but dismisses it just as quickly. I really hope my hand won't have to be forced into marrying her off to someone she doesn't want.

"Pity," Alexander says.

Fourteen

Alexa

"**G**irl, you got packages at your door, and they're kind of heavy," Jenna yells from somewhere down the hall.

"I do?" I ask, jumping up from my bed.

"Yeah." Jenna comes in with two matte-black packages topped with orange bows.

"What's in them?"

"Fuck if I know. Let's open them."

I give her a pair of scissors and let her go to town. She's far more interested than I am.

I've had more roses show up on my porch, and now I'm worried they're upping their game.

Black embossed tissue paper is neatly folded with a note on the top. She pushes the box toward me, but I shake my head. "You can open it. I don't like surprises."

"Again, where's your sense of adventure?" Jenna says, plucking the note off the top and reading it.

"Alexa, you're cordially invited to a Halloween party on October 31st. Wear this outfit and prepare to act like the angel I know you're not. I can't wait to see you, angel baby. P.S. this is not a request." Jenna snorts. "You naughty girl... Is this from that guy at the club?"

"Duh, I'm not sure of any other guys currently driving me crazy. He's the owner of said club, which makes it worse."

I haven't seen him in the past week and a half—since dining in the dark. Besides his consistent morning and nightly bossy texts, he's been MIA. I thought he was losing interest. I guess not.

Jenna pulls out a small black dress, angel wings, and a gold headpiece that looks eerily similar to something I've worn before.

"What the hell is that?" I regard the outfit with trepidation.

"An angel costume. Dummy."

"Yeah, I know what it is. I'm not wearing it."

"But it'll look adorable on you, angel baby," she teases.

"You're unbelievable and I'm not going."

"Well, let's open the other. Maybe he's giving you two options."

She opens the other with just as much enthusiasm. This box has the same tissue paper and another card. She reads it with scrunched brows.

"What a dick! No half-cute, half-sexy message for yours truly? Just a Jenna, you're cordially invited. Make sure Alexa shows up." Her face scrunches in disgust as she points to her chest. "I'm a main character too, goddammit, not a side ohhh—" She holds up a green outfit.

"What is it?"

"Poison Ivy, obvi."

"And you're happy about it?"

113

"Duh, she's kick-ass... although it could use a wig, because hello." She points at her scalp. "Blond hair is a no-go. Maybe some green jewels for around the eyes too. Yeah, I think that will do. Oh, and then makeup. We will, of course, have to go shopping. Then there are the shoes."

I continue to let her ramble. I want no part of the night she's planning.

She stops and looks over at me. "Hey, what's wrong? We can switch if you'd like, although I think I'm more of a Poison Ivy type."

"And what makes you think I couldn't pull off Poison Ivy?"

"Seductive, sarcastic, and loves plants? Come on, that has me written all over it. You're much more the angel type. Spiritual." She points at my neck. "You have crystals. You're sweet and meek. Although I might take back the last part after reading his note." Her smile nearly touches her ears as she fans herself.

"I can't with you, I swear."

"You love me, though." She blows me a kiss before placing her hands in a praying motion.

"Fine. An hour and then we're gone."

"Deal!" She grabs her costume and holds it up to herself in the mirror before leaving.

I wish I could share her enthusiasm, but the parallels between this life and my last are blurring and become similar in so many ways.

Too many coincidences equals trouble.

Fifteen

Gage

I watch Alexa as she applies the finishing touches to her angel costume. The disgust on her face is clear, even from the grainy video in her dark bedroom.

Alexa remembers the night of that college party differently from the way I remember it. She's missing many details that would alter her impression of the events of that night. She must think of it as the night Marco finally grew some balls and made the move on her. Little does she know I gave her the moment we both enjoyed. I'm the one who gave her the kiss she's always hoped for. Not the idiot who was busy getting head in an upstairs room while she was down waiting for him like the good girl she is.

Tonight, I have to tell her the truth. Wires are getting crossed, too many loose ends intermingling. Everything is going to implode if I don't start being honest.

Rosie moved in with me a week ago after some shit went down with Vic. I've made an exception and invited Rosie to my club tonight. I still haven't told her I've been talking to Alexa, and they'll be in close quarters tonight. Once she discovers I've been hiding it from her, she'll be furious, but I needed time. Time that is running out.

I should also take the devil costume off and trade it for Cupid since I'm giving Vic his one and only pass with Rosie tonight. The poor fuck fell for her and fucked it all up. Never did I think asking my best friend to watch over my little sister would turn into them falling for each other. Although, according to Vic, his emotions for her have run deep for many years. I don't like it, but I also trust him more than anyone else. If I had to choose anyone for her to be with, it would be him, even though I'm still fucking pissed at him. If everything goes well and Rosie is happy to see him and still loves him like I think she does, we'll write up the contract for them to be married. Then she'll be safe, which will be one less thing for me to worry about.

Alexa looks in the mirror one more time before her friend, Jenna, comes in wearing her costume. Bingo. Her friend took the bait, too.

Rosie descends the stairs in her glittery costume, revealing more skin than I would have preferred my baby sister to wear.

"You look pretty, Ro," I say as I hastily hide my phone in my pocket.

"Thanks. I'm glad you talked me into going out."

I sense uncertainty and sorrow in her voice. "Everything will work out. I promise you," I say, understanding that she doesn't grasp my meaning, but she will shortly.

"Yeah, well, I don't know if getting my heart stomped on was supposed to happen, but I'll take your word for it," she says as she walks past me.

"Not everything is as it seems. Just give it time." She gives me a quizzical expression before rolling her eyes. I swear, even grown, she's a pain in the ass.

As we make our way into the club and to my office, I see all the boys waiting for me. Most are Vic's biker brothers. I'm paying them a small fortune for their services tonight. They're donned in head-to-toe black carnival masks. Anonymity is something we enjoy having in this club and for tonight, they will need to be anonymous to the girls. As I speak to them, Rosie sits off to the side, on my couch. She looks around since this is the one and only time she will be allowed in this establishment.

Vic can't keep his eyes off her, and he's going to mess it up before he even gets close to her. I continue with my plans for tonight, keeping them brief and in code so Rosie doesn't get wind of the situation. The boys already understand they need to keep Poison Ivy entertained so I can have my moment with my angel. I don't want a repeat of the last time. Vic is on Rosie detail. God help him... or not. I'm still pissed off at him.

The boys head out, and I have a word with Vic before calling Rosie over.

"This will be your security for the night. Act as if he doesn't exist." I smirk. Rosie looks a little unsure of him, rightfully so with the mask, but ignores him, much to my pleasure.

"Can I go enjoy my night now? The dance floor and a drink are calling my name," she huffs out.

"Stay in the bar area and take it easy on the alcohol." The last thing I want is for her to stumble upon any of the remaining sections of the club.

"I will," she says, looking a little flushed and queasy. "But last I checked, you're not Papa, and I can drink what I want, when I want." She stomps out of the room without a second glance.

"She's all yours," I tell Vic, knowing she won't make it easy on him whatsoever. I watch him waste no time coming up on her heels.

I take a moment to collect myself in the silence of my office. My thoughts are all over the place. My stomach can't help but have knots of uncertainty. Unsure of how the next couple of hours will play out, of how Alexa will be.

In her presence, I'm unwaveringly confident behind my mask, but in my mind, the fifteen-year-old boy still clings to the thought that I'll be cast aside once again. She's the only person who has the power to turn me into the boy of my past.

I spot her on my screen as soon as she enters the club.

Donning a mask, I make my way into the bar area, where the vibrant costumes of the packed crowd catch my eye.

I sent Alexa a text earlier, instructing her to venture through the black door positioned on the right side of the bar alone.

Tonight, she will not only witness but take part in another section of the club, and I'm practically buzzing with excitement.

She says something to Jenna before walking off in the direction I instructed while the boys intercept her friend since Jace is busy being the DJ after the one I had canceled.

There's also Vinny. I would have placed him on Alexa's friend, but I instructed him to keep my idiot twin preoccupied. I don't need him sniffing around here tonight. Vinny's also Alexa's cousin, and it would be unfortunate if she noticed him before she knew the truth.

I watch my dark angel walk to the door, scan her band, then disappear through the door. I count to ten, my heart pounding in my chest, before silently trailing her. As I enter, I notice her scanning the dimly lit hallway with a nervous gaze, as if expecting someone to be lurking in the shadows.

Hanging above the next door is a neon sign that shines brilliantly, beckoning you to step into *Wanderland.* Many clients come to the club specifically for the primal play experience, seeking an exhilarating and uninhibited escape. Something I have yet to experience until now.

Just as she's about to walk through the threshold, she turns back and her eyes meet mine. From just a few steps away, I can hear her gasp in surprise. A small smirk plays on my lips as my cock hardens.

"Run, piccolo angello."

She pauses for mere seconds.

I take a deliberate step forward, showing my intentions.

She turns back and rushes through the door.

I take my time, as this area is off-limits to everyone tonight besides my girl and me.

Sixteen

Alexa

"**R**un, piccolo angello."

An exhilarating shriek leaves my lips before I'm running through the door and into a... forest? My steps falter as I take everything in. The room is dark, illuminated by a full moon, which is round, large, and fake. On this Halloween night, the moon outside is a slender crescent and not as bright.

The air is chilly in here, making goose bumps rise on the exposed skin not covered by my costume, and it even smells woodsy in here. I would believe I was in a forest if I was blindfolded and unaware of my location before entering. As far as the eye can see, there is an endless expanse of trees, while the floor is covered with a layer of dirt, gravel, and leaves.

I take off straight into the trees. I can't hear the devil so intent on chasing me, but I sense him just as I feel the pounding of my heart. His presence is somewhere nearby, lurking in the shadows, patiently biding his time for the perfect opportunity to strike.

My breath comes in ragged gasps from a combination of exhaustion from running and the excitement at the thought of being caught by him.

I turned my head to the right, only to be met with an eerie void of darkness. The sound of a branch snapping up ahead to my left startles me, making me pause for a moment.

Shit.

I dash to the right, my heeled feet pounding against the ground in rapid succession. A soft giggle escapes from the depths of my throat. I'm enjoying this far too much.

What kind of twisted person is he creating in me?

A towering tree trunk catches my eye, offering a perfect hiding spot. As I crouch behind it, I place my hand over my chest with a smile.

"Where are you, baby?" His deep voice carries from the other side of the tree.

My palm slams against my mouth, attempting to muffle the squeak on the verge of breaking free.

His retreating steps echo in the silence. I wait a minute, then two, listening intently to the rustling leaves before glancing around the tree.

Nothing.

Slowly, I make my way toward what I think is the entrance, guided by the soft glow of the artificial moon, with the cool shadows of the trees above me.

A searing sensation grips my back as I'm pulled by the wings of my costume and land straight into his hard chest.

With a firm hold, he wraps his arms around me, his lips grazing my earlobe, sending shivers down my spine.

"Mine," he says deep and breathlessly.

Our ragged breaths echo in perfect harmony. I feel the hardness of his cock pressed against my back, causing me to wriggle within his grasp as I squeeze my thighs together. His touch is electrifying as his hand journeys down my hip, lifting the hem of my dress and sending shivers of delight through my body as he stimulates me through the sheer material of my thong.

"You're soaking wet for me," he rumbles as he pulls them to the side and rubs his fingers up and down my slit. "You craved the chase, yet you longed for me to capture you."

He removes his hand and spins me around to face him. My gaze is drawn to his unsettling devil mask, a striking combination of red and black, with two horns protruding from the top and concealing his entire face.

This is the first time I've been this close to seeing him.

Slowly, I extend my hand toward the mask, but he shakes his head in refusal while gripping my hand.

My brows furrow. "Why can't I see you?"

"What if you don't like what you see?"

There's no way I won't like what I see.

"Let me be the judge of that."

His head shakes once again, revealing the obvious conflict raging within his thoughts. The only things that catch my attention are his deep-blue eyes, which convey gentleness, contradicting his outward appearance.

"You can't kiss me with the mask on," I say with a shy smile.

I wait while he contemplates his next words. "Close your eyes." The vulnerability is apparent in his voice.

I pause at his sudden change. "Why?"

"Because I said so," he says gruffly.

"Fine," I mutter, shutting my eyes.

"Good girl," he whispers with his lips lingering just inches from mine.

"Remember," he whispers as his lips brushing against mine, "this is what you wanted."

His confusing words linger in my mind for a fleeting moment while I become entranced by his presence. My mouth opens first, and I relish the sensation of my tongue caressing his. I can feel the warmth of his touch as he wraps both hands around my back and lifts me, our bodies becoming one.

My fingers dig into his back, aching to pull him nearer as if the distance between us is unbearable.

He breaks the kiss and rests his head against mine. "You drive me fucking crazy. You know that? So fucking crazy."

His lips explore the side of my neck, leaving a trail of kisses and gentle sucking. A moan escapes my lips as I surrender to the sensations, tilting my head to the side to give him better access. Goose bumps replace the warmth of his lips.

"Please," I whimper.

"What do you want?" he asks against my neck.

"Fuck me." The words fall from my lips so easily for him.

I should care that I don't know his name, I should care that I haven't seen his face, but I don't. I want this and I want him.

"Are you sure?"

"Yes."

He releases his arm wrapped around my waist, and with a sudden tug, he tears the delicate lace thong off from the back with a resounding rip before taking large strides with me still in his arms.

"No, in here. I don't want to leave yet."

"Okay," he says as he leans us both against a tree.

I gaze upward, my smile widening as I take in the sight of the faux trees forming a dark canopy above us. I can't believe I'm finally doing this. My heart races with a mix of excitement and nervousness.

The sound of his belt buckle jingling fills the air as he tenderly explores my neck while bringing his cock to my entrance.

"Look at me, Alexa."

Upon hearing my name from him for the first time, an instant surge of familiarity and a profound sense of connection washes over me.

I gaze into the very blue eyes belonging to someone I know all too well, just as he thrusts up into me.

My scream pierces the silence of the fake forest, fueled by both the sudden realization of who stands before me and the searing pain radiating from between my legs.

"Fuck!" he says breathlessly. "Are you—"

My world spins and crumbles into a million pieces.

"Put me down," I say as tears form behind my eyes.

I think I'm going to throw up.

With a gentle lift, he raises me before carefully setting me back on my feet and stepping away.

Gage stands tall, his broad shoulders cast a large shadow over me. There's a noticeable change in his appearance since I last saw him, but his eyes remain unchanged, full of warmth and the familiarity I'd cling to if not for the immense pain of betrayal.

"Why... why would you—?" A tear cascades down my cheek, leaving a salty taste on my lips. "How could you?"

The sensation of a crushing pressure on my chest leaves me gasping for air.

He lied to me. He played me. He tricked me.

"You—you've been the one this whole time and we just—" I can't even finish a fucking sentence.

In the midst of my world collapsing, he stands there motionless, deep in contemplation.

I take a step back and then another. I have to get the fuck out of here. As I flee from the devil, the same sense of urgency that gripped me upon entering persists, yet the exhilaration has faded, leaving only a profound sense of dread and sorrow.

The exit is like a beacon of light, illuminating over a door, and I eagerly head toward it. In a rush, I burst through the door and welcome the vibrant lights and energetic atmosphere of the club.

I scan the room, my eyes darting from corner to corner, desperately searching for Jenna. When I don't see her, I say fuck it and run to the front entrance.

My thighs are sticky, and I don't need to touch them to understand I'm a bloody mess from where Gage just took my virginity.

What the hell did I do?

Out of nowhere, someone wearing a shimmering silver costume walks up to me, and I have to fight back the urge to burst into tears. It's Rosie. Her words reach my ears, but they are drowned out by the chaos in my mind.

She becomes my lifeline as I grasp onto her just as Jenna rushes our way. I sense Gage's presence looming behind me, but I resist the urge to glance backward.

I can't.

Seventeen

Gage

Vic runs up next to me as we bolt through the front entrance. The bouncers eye me dubiously, but I disregard them. I hear a screech of tires right before I see the girls driving away.

"Motherfucker!" I yell into the air.

"What the fuck happened?" Vic asks.

"She ran when she figured out it was me," I say as I massage my temples.

The other guys run out, but I ignore them and make my way into my office with Vic, Trey, Marcus, and Julian on my heels.

I need to know how badly I fucked things up and devise a plan to fix it.

Finally, the monitor shows all three of them sitting cross-legged on Alexa's bed, with wine and food. They sing off-key to some song while all five of us are huddled around the monitors like a bunch of fucking weirdos.

"Okay, spill. Who was that guy earlier? He looked upset when you left," Alexa says to Rosie.

"It's a long, shitty story." Rosie sighs.

My eyes narrow as I fix Vic with a venomous look, but he just looks at the screen as if I don't exist, waiting for Rosie's next words.

"Spill, Rosalinda," Alexa says.

"Don't you dare full name me, Alexandria."

"How dare you!" Alexa screams, and then they laugh.

"Fuck, these girls are drunk as fuck. It's giving me a headache," Trey mutters behind us.

"Leave then," Vic says, eyes still glued to the screen.

"Not until I hear Poison Ivy's voice again," Trey says. Interesting.

"Shit!" Alexa jumps up and looks around. "Cameras."

"Fuck. She remembered." I sigh, though I doubt they'll find them.

"Fucking Gage. He put cameras in my room before I knew it was him," Alexa seethes.

"So you were putting on little shows for the devil?" her friend Jenna says, wiggling her eyebrows.

"She's fucking perfect," Trey murmurs.

"What? No! I was flipping him off most of the time."

"Rightfully so. That's creepy as hell!" Rosie says, looking around, pissed and disgusted by my activities.

Jenna jumps up. "Do you know where they are?"

She looks around Alexa's room as if she can find them. Fat chance, blondie.

"If I did, I would've already gotten rid of them, genius."

"It's actually funny. This chick thinks she'll be able to find them," Trey says from behind as he moves closer to the screen.

She nods before continuing her search. "Right... Be right back."

"Where the fuck is Poison Ivy going?" Trey leans in to get a better look at the other monitors.

Jenna runs back into the frame moments later with something in her hands. We all move closer to the screen and squint.

"Sorry, boys!" Jenna says before my screens go black.

"What the fuck just happened!" Vic yells as I try to bring the feed back up.

"Fuck if I know. She couldn't have found them," I say as I type into my computer, but it's futile. The signal is lost.

"Must have been some sort of scrambler," Julian mutters. "I'm impressed."

"It seems Poison Ivy is more formidable than I originally thought," Trey says as he walks to the door. "We'll be in touch," he says before the three walk out.

Changing gears and attempting to get my mind off the cluster fuck I created, I glance at Vic. "Everything's set if you're ready to take the plunge."

"I'm ready, but with a couple of changes from our original agreement."

"Like?" I ask, confused.

We already agreed that Vic gets Rosie, but he and the motorcycle club pledge to me and they're now part of my outfit. It will keep them safe, Vic free from ever getting locked up again, and it will also keep Rosie safe. It's a win-win for everyone involved.

"I want her to be free from this life and me. I want her to have a fresh start."

"Are you out of your fucking mind?"

He snorts. "Probably, but her happiness is more important to me. Freedom is what she's always wanted. I want to give her that."

Just as I'm about to tell him he's a fucking idiot for letting Rosie go, a sudden knock interrupts me.

"You rang..." Marco's tennis shoes squeak against the floor, announcing his arrival. His tight white tennis outfit and racket are an obnoxious sight, while Vinny reluctantly follows him and looks as if he'd rather be anywhere but here.

Vic looks at him with disgust. He's been on my side since the beginning. Even offering to take him out. I'm tempted, but I need him, unfortunately.

"Easy... we're going to be brothers after all," Marco says while holding his hand and racket up in surrender with a smile.

"Baby bro, nice outfit. I'm shocked the costume still fits."

His comment throws me off track, but I act unfazed. The fucker knew I was trailing him, but he always acted so aloof. I guess he isn't as stupid as I thought.

"I guess we both like to use the same shit two years in a row," I tell Marco.

"Ahh... I was wondering how you knew what I was going to wear that night."

So he only knew I followed him when he took Alexa and Rosie, not the year before.

"I must say, you jumped on her pretty quickly that night. Was it because you saw her get on her knees for me in her dorm?" Marco grins. I'm going to kill this motherfucker. The image of her pleading on her knees that night in her dorm still makes me nauseous.

"And you," Marco utters as he glances at Vic. "I gave you your time with Rosie that night, too. So perhaps ease up on the hostility."

"Fuck you," Vic spits.

"Are you always this fucking grouchy?" Marco asks Vic, who pointedly ignores him.

"Let's fucking do this," I say, checking my watch. I need to get this shit over with so I can figure out my next moves with Alexa.

Vic, who was once a member of The Demented Devils MC, until he got arrested for illegal activities, spills all the details about my father's connection to the club. It turns out my father was the one who tipped off the authorities to save my reckless brother after one of his many fuckups during our high school years. Marco, with a sense of decency, keeps his head down and remains silent as Vic divulges everything. This comes as a relief, especially since he's mainly responsible for our incarceration.

Vic leaves first as he needs to get more information from Trey, who's now the president of the MC after his father stepped down a while back.

"Bye, brother!" Marco yells after him, but Vic tells him to fuck off as he exits.

"He's going to end up killing you if you don't dial it the fuck back." I sigh, already tired of his shit and ready for him to leave.

"Nah, he doesn't want to upset Rosie," he mutters as he swings the racket around like an idiot.

"You know, she only needs one brother; we can get rid of one of the copy and paste."

"You're creepy as fuck since getting out," he mutters.

"It would be best for you to remember that."

"Noted. I spoke to Alexa's father, as you instructed."

"And?" I ask.

"I thought I wouldn't make it out of his house alive. He knocked me out from behind right after I rang the doorbell. I woke up in his basement, chained to a fucking wall. He waterboarded me within an inch of my life. I probably still have water in my lungs."

"Don't be so dramatic." I smirk.

I knew Mr. Rossi wouldn't take it easy on him, and the awareness that he didn't gives me sick satisfaction. Alexa's dad is a wolf in sheep's clothing. He can be fucking unhinged for those he loves. Let's just hope he doesn't do the same to me because of tonight's fuckup.

"He's ready to speak with you. Good luck," Marco says with a laugh as he leaves.

I sit across from Mr. Rossi in his home office. Floor-to-ceiling shelves with thousands of books and artifacts litter the area. It reminds me of something a history professor would have in college on a movie or television show.

He also has the temperament of an educator if you're fortunate enough to stay on his good side. I've always respected him for the father he is, almost as much as I respect the boss he is.

His office doesn't intimidate me or cause me anxiety, as my father's office once did, but I'm still on edge.

There's a tightness in my chest that's hard to ignore. I loosen my tie and take a sip from my glass of red wine, hoping to ease some of it.

The solid oak doors creak open, and I gaze into the eyes of the reason for the tightening in my chest.

I haven't spoken to Alexa since Halloween, six nights ago. Though I've tried multiple times.

Alexa stops dead in her tracks. Her eyes are wide, and her face pales slightly.

"Princess, come. Take a seat," her father says as he waves to the unoccupied wingback chair next to mine.

She walks as if she's going to her execution. Her eyes stay solely focused on her father, without even a passing glance in my direction. It fucking hurts, but it gives me the opportunity to stare at her. The black long-sleeved sheath dress hits mid-calf and hugs her curves in all the right places. It's the most modest I've ever seen her, and I'd be lying if it didn't make me a little hard imagining what she has on underneath.

As she goes to sit, she deliberately moves the chair farther away from mine, causing a sharp pang in my chest.

"Why did you want me here?" Alexa asks her father.

"Gage came to propose an alliance between the two families."

"What type of alliance?" she asks with wide eyes.

"An arranged marriage."

Dead fucking silence fills the room. Her father glances over at me before looking back at her.

"I realize this must come as a shock to you. Seeing Gage for the first time after so long."

She nods. "You could say that."

"What do you think?" he asks her.

"About what?"

Ouch.

"The arranged marriage."

"Do you think it would be best?" Alexa asks him in a small voice.

"I think it would benefit you both," he says with a nod.

My breath hitches in my throat and a knot forms in my stomach as I wait for what feels like an eternity for her reply.

"Very well. If you believe it will be best. I'll do it," she says before rising and walking out without another word or glance my way.

Eighteen

Alexa

With hesitance and apprehension, I cautiously step into Gage's club. Memories of Halloween a week ago flood my mind, replaying the moment I learned the truth.

"Pursuit of Happiness" blasts through the speakers around the club as if there are a hundred people and not just the two of us. If not for that, I'm sure I'd hear my erratic heart pounding in my ears, matching the sensation of it thumping inside my chest.

The club is dark aside from the red lights illuminating behind the bar and the ember from the blunt currently hanging between Gage's fingers.

He looks at home, in his kingdom of decadence and debauchery, while occupying one couch with his arms spread wide across the backrest. He points his head toward the heavens, though he reigns in the underworld below.

He's the new boss of Chicago, after all. Something I haven't quite come to terms with, or maybe I haven't come to terms with the fact that I begrudgingly agreed to marry him yesterday. I was unaware of what awaited me when my dad summoned me to his office. I knew it was something serious since we never meet in there.

What I didn't expect was to see Gage sitting across from my dad. I felt blindsided by them, but it's not like Dad was aware that Gage and I had already had our dumpster fire of a reunion. And worse, when my dad mentioned the marriage, I said yes, ignoring the screams in my head.

The thought of disappointing my dad is not an option for me. I'm determined to make him proud, and if it means a marriage I don't want, so be it.

My heart hurts at the thought of the clinical and callous way I'm thinking about something that once made me smile. I wanted to have a blissful marriage like my parents have always had, with someone I can lean on when times get hard. Someone to be my best friend and partner.

I don't know this new person in front of me, but a strong intuition tells me he possesses the ability to handle tasks effectively and fill in the gaps where I fall short. That's what brings me here today.

I stop in my tracks, unsure if he's noticed my presence.

He draws the blunt between his lips and inhales deep before blowing the billowing smoke out of his lungs and angling his head down toward me. Smoke covers his face before it dissipates into nothingness and all that's left is his handsome face. The face that used to bring me solstice and warmth now brings me uncontrollable shivers of uncertainty and irritation, but worse, desire.

I rub my hands down my arms at the sudden chill and then stop. He doesn't need to know his effect on my emotions.

A sense of safety still clings to me from this distance, yet, as soon as our eyes meet, I can feel the weight of his stare, a palpable heat that seems to strip away my clothes.

My blood boils with a need I've never associated with him before.

His eyes are unwavering as he takes a final, lingering drag from the blunt. The smoke curls around his face before he snuffs it and stands.

My instincts scream for me to take a step back with each advancing step he takes, but I hold my ground. His steps are leisurely, as if knowing his time with me is infinite and he'll catch me.

This man used to be my best friend. Then he disappeared without a trace, only to return as a different person entirely.

No longer is he the boy who held a piece of my heart.

The one who made me playlists and held me when I felt sad.

No longer is he sweet, understanding, and quiet.

He's everything dark, deviant, and calculating.

His sights aren't set on being my friend again.

No, he wants everything I have to give and more.

He wants to own every piece of me.

It's hard to reconcile the man standing in front of me as Gage, my best friend, the boy I loved, and the man in front of me now. A man who's been messing with me. Playing with me. Stalking me. Lying to me. They feel as if they're two separate entities. The man in front of me needs a different name. He isn't who he claims to be.

He's in a suit that fits him to perfection. Black dress pants hang low on his hips, his suit jacket is off, and his white dress-shirt sleeves are rolled up to his elbows, showing off extensive tattoo ink. He's much bulkier than I remember. His muscles now have muscle as if stacked.

I felt so idiotic when I didn't realize who he was, but how could I? He's different now. In both personality and appearance. Even his voice is deeper and graver than I remember it being.

I take two steps back because I can't handle it any longer.

"Stop retreating, piccolo angello," his gruff voice says over the music as he advances on me.

"Stop calling me that!" A wave of irritation washes over me. If he thinks we've returned to the pre-Halloween dynamic, he's delusional.

I swallowed my pride and pushed down the hurt to come here today so we could talk and reach an understanding. Since we're now engaged, we must project an image of strength and unity; any sign of weakness will be exploited by our enemies.

I didn't come here to be chased through his fake forest or be called his little pet names.

"Calling you what?" He asks with a predatory gleam in his eyes.

"Little Lamb," I say breathlessly as I glance back and realize that in my preoccupied state, I've moved away from the entrance and further into the club.

When I look back at him, he's even closer to me.

"But that's what you are," he murmurs as he rubs the back of his fingers along my cheek. "My little lamb, and I'm the big bad wolf waiting to devour you. Claim you for eternity, like I should have done all those years ago."

"You're delusional."

"Am I?" He asks with a tilt of his head.

My insides heat, and a ball of emotion gets stuck in my throat. My instincts tell me to run, but the burning in my core has other ideas altogether. I hate him for how he makes my body want him, even when I'm pissed at him.

My back hits the wall with a thud as I inch myself into a very dark corner. It's a very precarious and idiotic situation to put myself in.

He is a wolf hunting me, as he says. The dark, predatory gleam in his eyes shows me how delighted he is. The intoxicating smell of his cologne mixed with the earthy aroma of marijuana leaves me unsteady. His body inches even closer to mine as I drive my body further into the curtains adorning the walls.

With his lower lip clenched between his teeth, Gage inches his right hand closer to my face. I close my eyes, not from fear, but because his gaze overwhelms me. Then, I feel his thumb delicately tracing the curves of my lips.

His earlier words do not resonate with his current actions. He's being gentle and sweet—something I would have experienced with the Gage from before.

"This is the way it should have always been. You were only ever meant for me."

My throat constricts as I swallow, and my eyes, glistening with unshed tears, flutter open. My earlier resolve comes back to me full force. The reason for coming to meet him today runs through my mind like a smack across the face.

Halloween comes rushing back, the chase, the revelation, the pain.

He withheld his identity from you.

He broke into your house; he played with you.

He lied to you.

I swat away his hand from my face.

"We might have to get married, but make no mistake, it will be a marriage of convenience and nothing more. I don't like this new Gage."

He takes a step back as if giving me the space I need as an expression I've never seen crosses his features before it disappears, and a wicked grin emerges.

My stomach does a somersault.

Jesus, what the hell is wrong with me? Why does my body enjoy this side of him so much?

He tsks. "The Gage you once knew died the second my brother, the one you were so intent on marrying, fucked me over." He grabs the necklace he gave me that hangs around my neck from between my breasts. He holds it as if it's a priceless treasure before grasping the chain and turning until he looks at the engraved date.

"You will be mine. All of you," he says before laying it back against my skin.

I watch his retreating form as he walks away without a backward glance, my breathing ragged from the encounter.

He isn't the same Gage, but what he doesn't understand is, I'm not the same Alexa either.

That evening, I zip up my skintight black dress, followed by my highest pointy-toed red high heels.

Jenna looks at me as she sits cross-legged in the middle of my bed. "Why are you doing this, anyway? Yes, Gage was a complete and total bag of dicks, but I don't think this is the best idea."

"I second that," Rosie says from the doorway. "You were pretty upset when you got home from talking to him earlier. Maybe you should wait."

"I can't." I sigh. "Gage thinks I'm just going to roll over and do whatever he wants, like before. Now that he's technically my boss, I need to show him it will only be business between us. Arranged marriage or not."

Rosie winces. "You're playing with fire, but I'm behind you all the way."

"Hear, hear," Jenna cheers. "Who's the guy, anyway?"

"His name's Brad. He's from accounting at work."

"Yawn. Sounds like a total fucking snooze fest, if you ask me," Jenna says.

"I didn't ask you," I say as I apply my red lip stain and then glance at her in the mirror's reflection. "And who are you to talk with all of your secret outings lately? Don't think I haven't noticed you being gone all week."

She shrugs. "It was just a bunch of errands for work."

"Yeah, sure."

Jenna rolls her eyes. "So, after your date with Mr. Dull, who probably wears socks during sex and drives a Prius, what do you plan on doing? Because I'm thinking of drinks and more drinks to celebrate our girl's special day tomorrow." Jenna points at Rosie.

"I'll be back later tonight, and then we'll drink and eat our weight in junk food. I'm sorry we didn't do more for your bachelorette party."

"It's not safe to be out and about. Besides, I'm happy just having you girls to hang with tonight," Rosie says.

"My date is early enough that I should be back no later than nine."

Jenna snickers. "Brad, the bore, chose the early date? What? Past his bedtime?"

"No, I chose it so we could have girl time. He's been asking me out for weeks, and I always decline, but after earlier, I said fuck it. My temper was through the roof, and I had vengeful thoughts. I texted Brad, and he said he was free tonight," I say with a shrug.

"So he's kind of like a rebound," Jenna mutters.

"There's nothing to rebound from," I say, grabbing my bag.

We arrive at the upscale steak restaurant about twenty minutes later. Brad looks decent in his khaki slacks and button-down shirt. His blond hair is combed over to one side, and a pleasant smile sits on his lips. He takes my hand as he ushers me from his car, which happens to be a Prius— a detail that had Jenna snorting in laughter as he picked me up. His hand is a little clammy, which makes me grimace.

A small irritating voice in my head reminds me that Gage's hand wouldn't be clammy. If anything, it would only be strong, warm, and commanding. I roll my eyes and try to banish any thought of him away. This is about retaliation and showing Gage I won't give in as easily as he wants. This isn't about comparing the two men. So I decide to give Brad the benefit of the doubt. Maybe he's just nervous. But the promise to not compare lasts about two seconds. As we walk to the table, he holds the small of my back, and it feels all wrong.

I've never cheated, but the guilt consuming me mirrors my conception of a cheater's remorse. I could kill Gage for making me feel this way even though I'm not even with him. Yet. Technically.

My phone rings with a notification. I apologize and check it just in case it's Rosie or Jenna.

The Liar

> Why the fuck are you on a date with the stiff?

The Liar

> You're testing my fucking patience.

My eyes scan the restaurant briefly before I type out my reply.

Alexa

> Last I checked, you weren't my daddy or my man. Run along while I enjoy my date.

I can't help but smirk. He needs to experience a hint of the pain I felt when he lied to me. Maybe I'm being petty, but what did he expect? Me to jump into his arms once I found out? If so, he's not only delusional but insane.

The Liar

> You didn't seem to mind when you were cumming on my fingers and tongue. Leave the table and come outside.

Alexa

> I didn't know it was you when I came. So your point is pointless.

"Is everything okay?" Brad asks from the other side of the table.

Shit. I forgot where I was. Gage has a way of doing that to me.

I glance up at Brad as he gazes at me from above his menu. "Yeah, it's just my friend. Everything's good."

"Do you know what you want?"

"Umm..." I browse the menu and find the first thing my eyes see. "I'll just get the steak and potato puree."

"You wouldn't rather get something lighter?"

That has me looking up at him. I must have heard him wrong.

"Lighter? Like what?" I say ten seconds from getting pissed.

He shrugs. "Most girls would get a salad or soup."

I quirk a brow. "Well, this girl enjoys food."

Brad clears his throat before glancing back at the menu, clearly annoyed. The nerve of this fucking guy for berating my food choice. This is shaping up to be a shitty night, but I must commit to teach Gage a lesson.

My phone beeps again while Brad orders.

The Liar

> Pointless, huh? Stop with the games and come outside.

Alexa

> No, I don't think I will. Fuck off, Gage.

The Liar

> Okay

My smile vanishes. *Okay?*

It's never that easy with him. I scan the room again as if he'll materialize at another table or the bar. Nothing greets me. I shrug it off as I glance across the table at my date.

This was a huge mistake. I should be at home with my best friends. I pick up my phone and text a message to our girls' group chat to save me when I hear a grunt and direct my attention upward.

Brad scrunches his nose, and I almost let him have it for looking at me with disgust when I smell it, too. Something's burning.

A loud alarm cuts through the air, accompanied by a bright flashing white light, leaving everyone confused and searching for its source.

We're ushered outside by staff as I see a huge black cloud of smoke billow from the kitchen area.

I can't help but experience a little relief at the abrupt end of this disastrous date until I see Gage casually leaning against Brad's car. His legs and arms crossed, making his dark suit mold to his body in all the right places.

He looks like trouble. Someone poor Brad couldn't hold a candle to.

There are leagues, and there are planets, and Gage is on a different planet than Brad.

With a predatory focus, Gage assesses my date like a spider examining a fly caught in its web. A smirk curves his lips, much to my distaste. He's not worried in the least, which makes this night pointless.

"Gage, what are you doing here?"

"About to make s'mores. Heard they were having an unfortunate fire in the kitchen."

My eyes widen at the thought of him having something to do with the evacuation. He wouldn't intentionally start a fire to end my date, would he? I scan the mischievous grin on his face.

Yes, yes, he would.

"Do you know this guy?" Brad, oblivious to the looming danger of Gage, asks at my side.

"He's an old friend of my family," I mutter to piss Gage off.

Gage's eyes heat, and I know I've hit my mark. "Actually, she's going to be my wife."

"Not on your life."

"We'll see about that." Gage steers his eyes to Brad as he steps away from the car. "You can run along now. She'll be coming with me."

"No," Brad says abruptly. "She doesn't seem like she wants to, and we haven't finished our date."

Gage raises an eyebrow before chuckling under his breath. He takes the two remaining steps until he's in Brad's face. To Brad's credit, he barely flinches.

I hold my breath, as a strange combination of uncertainty and apprehension churn in my stomach. I have yet to encounter this side of Gage, and I don't know how to navigate it.

"You see, that's where you're wrong," Gage looks down at me, licking his bottom lip before trapping it between his teeth and then releasing it. "She chose that tight-as-fuck dress with me in mind. She knew it would be me ripping it off later," he says without breaking eye contact with me.

My body is on fire. Gage knows what his words do to me. Even though I don't want it to, it pulls me into his devious web.

The air buzzes with a palpable tension as our eyes lock, a silent struggle between us, but poor Brad, stuck in the middle, serves as an unintentional buffer, making our awkward silence even more strained.

"Fine. You can have the whore," Brad retorts.

His words make me cringe, more for his sake than my feelings. He's unaware of our world or who he's challenging.

Gage's head snaps to Brad. "What the fuck did you just say?"

The air around us shifts a few degrees lower as Gage's mood takes a nosedive.

Realizing his error, Brad backpedals, trying to correct his words. In the next second, Gage's grip tightens around Brad's throat, suffocating the air from his lungs. Brad's face contorts into a horrifying mix of red and blue. Brad might deserve an ass kicking for his rude comment, but he doesn't deserve to die.

I grab Gage's arm, feeling the cords of muscle and raw rage burning through him. "Gage, stop, it's not worth it."

"Fuck that. No one speaks to you like that."

"Please!" I plead, surveying my surroundings, but the parking lot is deserted as the fire is on the other side of the building.

My anxiety grows as he continues to choke him. I don't want Gage to leave again for something like this.

I don't want him to leave me.

The thought sobers me.

I position myself between the two of them and meet a ticking jaw and a furious pair of eyes staring back at me. "Please, Gage," I whisper, my words barely audible as I nuzzle my face against his chest and cling to his waist.

A loud thump echoes in the air, followed by Gage's arms wrapping around me. The thump must have been Brad. Hopefully, he's not dead.

We stand there, wrapped in each other's embrace until Brad's engine breaks the silence and fades into the distance.

Once the coast is clear, I glance up at Gage, irritated as hell. "Looks like I won't be going back to that job."

He takes hold of my hand and pulls me in what I'm assuming to be the direction of his car.

"First of all, fuck that piece of shit. Second, your job is by my side."

"No," I say as I pause in front of his blacked-out Mercedes.

Gage heaves out a sigh. "No, what?"

"No, to whatever idea you have of us. I'll run my dad's business, but I won't be doing it with you."

"You will, as my wife."

"No."

With a gleam in his eye, he corners me, his gaze intense and unwavering. His wall of a body presses me against the side of his car, sending a chilling sensation through my body.

Retrieving the necklace from between my breasts, he spins the chain with a mischievous smile.

"The date of our wedding," he says with a smug grin.

"You gave this to me way before I agreed to marry you," I say, looking at the date inscribed for a couple of weeks from now.

"Because I knew it would happen. Just accept it. Accept us." His eyes, filled with desperation, plead with me to accept our marriage and him, but I still have my doubts.

When I say nothing, Gage's hands snake around my neck and squeeze as his eyes bore into me. "There will never be anyone besides me. Accept that shit."

His lips, warm and insistent, crush against mine.

A better woman would have pushed him away, but I'm not a better woman.

I rest my hands against his muscular chest as I surrender to his tongue dancing against mine. As our kiss grows more urgent, his hands release my neck and find their way into my hair, where they grip the strands roughly.

A gentle moan escapes my lips as his knee presses against the sensitive space between my thighs. "That's it, baby. Let me give you what you need."

A dizzying, fluttering swarm of butterflies erupts within me as the weight of reality hits. This is the first time I feel Gage kissing me. Not the mystery man he was. Just Gage. And it feels phenomenal.

It makes every touch of his body against mine more intense.

"Well, Rosie, I guess she's safe from the fire we were so worried about. Or is she?" Jenna says from somewhere close.

My eyes spring open, and I attempt to push Gage away.

"Fuck off, you two. This only concerns her and me, and we aren't done yet," Gage says, gazing down at me.

"This is done," I say while trying to push him away.

"The fuck it is," Gage says as he goes in for another kiss.

"Give her to us, Romeo. We have festivities to attend to for your sister," Jenna says.

He must weigh her words because his face dips, and he pecks my lips before leaning in further. His soft lips rest against the shell of my ear. "This, us, will never be done."

Then, he pushes off the car, walks around to the driver's side, and leaves without saying another word while I stand here disoriented, confused, and hot as hell.

"How was your date?" Rosie teases.

"Yeah, where's good old Brian, or was it Brett?" Jenna asks.

"You," I say, pointing at Rosie, "are clearly spending too much time with her." I point at Jenna.

"I may have indulged in a few too many shots," Rosie laughs, a bubbly, slightly uncontrolled sound, followed by a hiccup.

I regard them as a girl runs up beside Rosie. Then I squint.

"Are you all in Batman pajamas?"

"We came to save you, Robyn." Jenna grins.

Then they all laugh as if her words are the funniest thing they've ever heard.

"How did you guys know to come get me?"

"You sent us a message in the group chat with the letters H-E-L. It didn't take a rocket scientist to figure out it meant help," Jenna says.

The group chat. I've never been more grateful. Who knows what I'd be doing with Gage right now if they hadn't come to save me.

I extend my arm out to Jenna. "Give me the car keys, psycho."

"I drove, and I haven't been drinking."

"And you are?" I say, observing the girl next to Rosie with auburn hair and a sweet smile in the same Batman attire.

"Jess, Rosie's friend."

"Welcome to the shit show, Jess," I say with a smile as we walk back to the car.

"Hey Jenna, do you have more wine and Batman pajamas?"

"I got you."

Nineteen

Gage

I take my seat in the front row next to Alexa. From here, I have a clear view of the dock that's transformed into an aisle, with Vic standing at the end. The grin on his face looks like he won the lotto or some shit.

I glance over at Alexa before placing my hand on her thigh and leaning into her ear.

"You look heavenly today."

Her surprise gaze drops to my hand before she lies her own atop mine, the sharp points of her crimson claws sinking into my flesh. A clear warning. One I won't heed.

"Thanks," she says before removing her hand from mine, which now carries indentions from her nails. She looks down at my hand on her thigh, sighs, and then gazes out at the lake without asking me to remove my hand. As if she knows it's useless to try.

Ever since we got here, she's tried to steer clear of me. The bitter taste of her rejection and hatred linger like a phantom pain, a constant ache that fuels my resolve to break through her defenses. I've waited years for her, and a little more time, even if it's agonizing, won't kill me... much.

"What colors are you going to want for our wedding?" I ask with a smile.

"Black."

"Black?" I quirk my eyebrow.

"I'll be in mourning, or maybe it'll be your funeral. Haven't decided." She shrugs.

Just as I'm about to reply, the song changes, and my sister comes into view. She looks beautiful and so happy. At least I got one thing right.

With a radiant smile that illuminates her entire face like sunshine, Rosie approaches Vic, her eyes fixated on his, as if none of us exist.

Will Alexa ever look at me that way? Or will she hate me forever?

I glance over at Alexa; a sweet smile plays on her lips, happy tears glistening in her eyes as she watches Rosie walk down the aisle to the gentle strains of the wedding march.

I hand her the pocket square of my suit. "It's not going to bite you. Although I think you'd like it," I say, close to her ear.

With narrowed eyes, she snatches the fabric from my grasp, then turns to watch my sister's final strides to Vic.

"Damn, baby bro, I'm starting to think she'd prefer me over you."

I whip my head the other way toward my stupid-ass clone.

"Careful, I'll slit your throat and console Mom at your funeral with a smile on my face."

His lips tilt into a smirk while keeping his face forward and holding Mom's hand. The fucker is good at playing the doting son.

As the ceremony unfolds, Alexa allows my hand to rest on her thigh, unaffected by the small circles I trace with my thumb. It's a small win.

A short time later, I survey the bustling reception, filled with lively conversations and laughter.

I text Jace, who is the DJ for the night, with my song request. He pulls out his phone and rolls his eyes like a child before changing the song.

I rise from my seat and button my suit jacket before stalking toward her. She's lingering by the bar, conversing with her friend Jenna, to deliberately keep her distance from me.

"Dance with me," I say, touching her elbow.

"I'm busy with Jenna."

"Actually, she's unbusy," Jenna says as she pushes her back and into me. "You kids have fun."

"That's not a word, and I'm going to kill you," Alexa tells Jenna as I pull her to the dance floor.

Despite her stiffness, I still pull her into my body. Her arms wind around my neck in an awkward embrace, but I don't allow that to deter me.

"Relax, it's just a dance," I say near her ear before I kiss her neck, eliciting a squeak from her.

As we dance under the twinkling lights, the melodies of one song seamlessly blend into another. I feel her body relax as she finally rests her head against my chest.

I choose to savor the moment in silence and not ruin it by speaking. Our conversations used to be filled with laughter, thoughtful exchanges and genuine connection. I miss that.

But the connection we've always shared still lingers, like a familiar melody playing softly in the background. My fuckups have caused it to fracture, but I'll do whatever it takes to mend it. I just need to create more memories like this with her—to remind her how good we are together.

"May I cut in?" Marco asks from behind me.

I'm going to kill him.

"Absolutely the fuck not," I bark without turning around.

Alexa grows still in my arms and it makes me hate him a little more. He always knows how to ruin a perfect fucking moment.

"It's fine," she says, pulling back with a smile and patting my chest as if she's trying to calm me down.

I grab his arm as he moves between Alexa and me. "If your hands travel anywhere I don't like, I'll cut your fingers off with a pair of rusted, dull pliers, then force you to live like that for the rest of your miserable life."

"Graphic, I dig it. No worries, baby bro," Marco says before whispering something to Alexa that makes her laugh.

He apparently has a death wish. *Why did I decide to wait for his punishment?*

Reluctantly, I turn and make my way toward my future father and mother-in-law. I kiss Alexa's mom on the cheek. "Beautiful as always, Mrs. Rossi."

"You're going to make my girl happy, right?" she asks, narrowing her eyes.

"I will, or die trying."

"That's what I like to hear. I'm going to leave you boys and go see your mom," she says before swaying away. She and my mother have been friends since they were children. They're both ecstatic about our arrangement. Let's just hope I can get Alexa to share the same sentiment.

153

"Why is that slimeball dancing with my daughter?" Mr. Rossi asks while looking over at where Marco and Alexa are dancing.

They're in deep discussion, and it gnaws on my nerves not to know what they're talking about.

"I'll keep an eye on it."

"You do that," he says in his no-nonsense tone. "Have all the necessary preparations been made for the wedding and the events that come after? I want to make this transition seamless for her," he says as he gazes over at Alexa, who's laughing at something Marco says.

I fucking hate it. Beneath a thin veneer of confidence, my insecurities lurk, ready to pull me under if I'm not careful.

"There has been a challenge to her right. She will need you to protect her."

"What do you mean?"

"On the night of her attack, she didn't achieve her first kill. I killed him," he murmurs.

I glance at Mr. Rossi, absorbing his words in silence.

Before we come of age and assume leadership, we must accomplish a series of tasks. High on the list is a kill.

I too was in disbelief when I got the news of her kill while in prison. Not because she lacks ability, but because her heart is pure.

"Nothing will ever happen to her."

Mr. Rossi nods.

"Managing both houses won't be easy for you. I have taught her all that I can, but there is still much more for her to learn."

"I can handle it."

"Don't fuck it up, or I'll kill you." I regard him, knowing this isn't an idle threat. He means every word.

"If I fuck it up, I'll let you."

"Good, I'm going to go get his slimy hands off my girl."

"My girl," I correct as I watch Mr. Rossi sweep in and take Alexa from Marco.

As I enter my father's office the following morning, the weight of our last conversation before my incarceration comes rushing back, filling the room with an overwhelming sense of suffocation. I remember pleading with my father. My voice trembled with fear and uncertainty as I begged him to reconsider his decision to make me turn myself in for a crime I didn't commit.

Today, only he will be subject to fear or uncertainty.

From afar, I've been observing my father since my release. With his gray hair, expanding waistline, and wrinkles, it's clear that time has left its mark on him.

"Gage," he says, his voice strained as he struggles to stand.

"You can stay seated. From what I hear, you aren't doing too well, Hector."

"Father. I am your father, and you will address me as such."

"I don't have a father," I say, surveying his office.

A heavy silence hangs in the air. When I was a child, I used to fear entering this room. His lessons were brutal, and while the scars are still visible on the outside, the ones on the inside have festered into an unforgiving beast.

"Is there a reason for your unexpected visit?"

"There is," I say as I grab a glass from his drink cart. Just as I'd been instructed countless times as a child, I pour three fingers of scotch.

I hand him his favorite drink that is now playing a part in his demise. The jaundice of his eyes and skin hints at the severity of his stage-four liver failure. His days are limited in more ways than one.

He examines the warm amber liquid in the glass, spinning it and inhaling the scent before raising it to his lips and shooting it back.

"You see, I started looking into old ledgers from decades ago and discovered things you should have destroyed if you had any fucking sense. Thankfully for me, you don't."

I unbutton my suit jacket and take a seat across from him.

"You employed the Demented Devils MC to run guns and blow for years, until you ratted them out to the feds. Landing Vic in jail, the same Vic who just married your only daughter," I say as I hear footsteps.

Vic comes in the door and closes it silently.

"Then, your precious older son kills someone while drinking and driving, and you pin the crime on me, sending me into the same cell as Vic. Only for me to get out and take over the business you were trying so hard to keep me away from." I glance over at my father, but he remains silent, his expression unreadable. Figures.

"Way too many coincidences, if you ask me," Vic says as he makes his way over to us while my father remains silent.

"I thought you'd say nothing. In fact, I expected it from someone as shitty as you are. Shitty father, shitty husband, shitty boss," I count on my fingers.

"Shitty father-in-law," Vic says from my side. "Your daughter sends her love, by the way."

My father narrows his gaze at Vic. "You were never supposed to end up with her. A total waste of a transaction, if you ask me."

"All I'm interested in is a name from the ledger," I say, rubbing the back of my head. Scars litter my body as a reminder of the day I almost lost my life. The sensation of the makeshift blades piercing my skin ruthlessly and repeatedly still lingers. If it wasn't for Vic, I'd be six feet under. "They received a wire transfer the day I was almost stabbed to death in prison. Not to mention a fuck ton of other times someone either got hurt or died."

"I can answer that," Marco says as he walks in the door.

"What the fuck are you doing here?" I ask over my shoulder.

"What, you thought you could have a party and not invite me? I followed our brother in." Marco points at Vic.

"I'm not your fucking brother."

"We can work on that," Marco smiles before looking over at our father. "Sorry, Pop, someone new is in charge now, and I must keep in step. Plus, you've always been a fucking dick," he says, before directing his attention back to me. "I'm assuming you're talking about Nohl?"

"Yeah, how'd you know?" I say, looking over at my brother.

"Secrets are my specialty, worth more than money, as you know," he says with a sigh. "After Pop sent you in, I started following him and going through his shit. I wasn't sure when we talked on Halloween night, but now I know for sure. He calls favors in to Nohl, which means zero in Russian by the way, when he wants someone taken care of in and out of the Mafia."

The mention of Russia tightens a knot of unease in my stomach. If Alexander Petrov was part of this I would hope he would mention it with our newfound partnership. This is something I'll have to figure out later.

Then, the rest of what Marco says filters in, and my head whips in my father's direction. "You're killing off people within the families? Are you fucking insane?" I gaze back at my brother. "How long has this been going on?"

"Since before we were born."

"Does anyone else know?"

My head is spinning right now at the information. I harbored suspicions, but the evidence never quite solidified into undeniable proof... until now.

"Nah, he kept his deplorable deeds under wraps."

"Anything else we need to know?" I ask, not taking my eyes off my piece-of-shit father. I knew he was dirty, but I didn't know he had it in him to kill off members of the organization that we consider family.

"Well, he attempted to kidnap Rosie." Vic jumps up from his seat.

"When?"

"It was during the time she was in that town with you," Marco says.

"I fucking knew it, you motherfucker. They almost broke her arm and nearly killed Jess!" Vic yells.

"She was to be brought back to me. Where she belongs," my father seethes, as if kidnapping his own daughter is low on the meter of bad things to do.

"And what if they decided not to hold up to their end of the deal and took her, or worse, killed her?" Vic questions as he moves closer to my father.

"It was worth the risk of getting her away from you."

"I'm going to fucking kill you," Vic snarls.

"Before anyone makes a move, there's more," Marco looks at our father. "He put a hit on Alexa's father. I was able to stop it, but shit wasn't cheap."

I massage my temples. The shit is just stacking up in front of me. "Anything else?"

"Uncle George... he had him killed."

I gaze over at my father. "You killed your twin brother? For what, exactly? He was a fucking saint."

When he says nothing, Marco continues. "Another hit was placed, but I haven't been able to figure it out yet. It was for a fuck-load of money."

"Fucking perfect," I mutter as I drag my palms down my face.

"Are you willing to help us out? One good deed before it all ends?" Marco asks our father.

When he stays silent, I decide I don't want to be in here, in this house, in this office, in his presence any longer.

"Did you bring everything?" I gaze at Vic as I rise from my seat, pull my jacket off, and fold it over the back of the chair.

A heavy duffel bag lands at my feet. The weight and contents clang ominously, a sound that raises my anticipation and sends a shiver of excitement through me, prompting me to roll up the sleeves of my dress shirt.

"You brought party favors?" Marco asks Vic.

"Only the best for your dear old dad," Vic says with a sadistic smile before unzipping the duffle and pulling out tools and rope.

My father's self-preservation finally kicks in as he jumps from his chair, surprisingly quick for a sick, dying man.

"I'll tell you everything you need to know," he gasps.

"Start talking."

"Once I'm somewhere far away and safe, I will tell you everything."

My laugh catches him off guard. "Good one. Tell me now, or you die."

"Not until I'm somewhere safe."

He won't tell me shit if he leaves here now. I know it, and so does he.

"Nah, I think I got all the answers I need." I smirk. "What about you, Vic? You need any more answers?"

"Nope, I'm leaving for my honeymoon in about two hours. We need to speed this up. I miss my bride."

"Marco?"

He stares at our father for a beat before shaking his head. "I'm good."

"How dare you do this to me! I gave you everything, Marco, everything! For you to fuck it all up," he says, spit flying from his mouth and his face red with anger.

"This is the first right decision I've made since the day I killed that person." He gazes over at me. "I tried to turn myself in, but he wouldn't let me. He said he'd send Rosie and Mom to the Stockade if I didn't fall in line."

My insides quake at the information. Marco was protecting them. He was going to send my mom and sister into the sex trafficking ring if Marco didn't go along with his plan? I clench and unclench my fists multiple times to get my fury under control.

The Stockade was the first business I set fire to after I saved all the women. It always made me sick when he would take Marco and me there in our teens. It was my father's highest income stream, so it was the cherry on top of the cake when I burned it to the ground.

I hand them the rope. "Tie his ass to the chair."

My father puts up a pathetic fight, just like the pitiful man he is.

"What's the matter? You had no problem testing torture tactics on us as children to strengthen us, as you liked to say. It's time you get to experience a taste of the hell you inflicted on us."

Marco attempts to cover his mouth, but I stop him. "I want to hear him scream. Hold his head back," I say, observing my father's terrified eyes. "A tooth for every year I was caged like a fucking animal."

Marco holds his head back by his forehead while I grab his lower jaw and chin.

I can't help but smirk as his gurgled screams pierce the air. It's a pleasant contrast to the agonized cries he used to extract from us.

I grab a pair of pliers from the array of tools Vic brought. My father struggles against our hold. His skin is flush with perspiration, and the putrid scent of urine fills my nostrils. *Disgusting.*

As I squeeze the grips, the sharp sound of his tooth cracking fills the air, signaling my cue to rip it out.

The hole releases a captivating shade of bright red, leaving a trail down the side of his mouth and onto his pristine white button-down.

His pleas and tears fall on deaf ears as I continue, not relenting until his mouth is nearly toothless and a river of red runs down his chin.

I glance at Vic, motioning for him to have his turn. He deserves this just as much as I do.

He walks around and grabs a heavy machete. "I'd like to make this painful, slow, and something that lasts for hours, but I have a flight to catch and children to make," he says with a light in his eyes I only see when he speaks of my sister.

I roll my eyes, the disturbing images of him and my sister that he conjures making me cringe, but I let him have his moment.

Vic grabs my father's wrist and places his hand on the desk. My father promptly places his fingers into a fist, no doubt knowing what's coming. Vic slams his hand on the mahogany wood desk repeatedly until he opens it up and his palm is flat.

"This isn't for me," Vic says as he looks into my father's eyes. "This is for the daughter who never got the father she deserved."

The machete whistles through the air before chopping off four fingers at once. Bright red blood squirts across his desk. Vic grabs a few mutilated fingers and crams them into my father's mouth, even as he attempts to spit them out. My father is shaking and looks to be on the cusp of passing out. The metallic smell of blood permeates the office.

I ought to have a twinge of remorse. However, only satisfaction is present.

Vic places the weapon on the table and grabs my father's shoulder, who is now fading fast and scarcely conscious. "It's been nice, Hector. I'll see you in hell." He gives both Marco and me a salute before walking out of the office.

"Fuck, remind me not to get on his bad side."

"You can leave, and I'll finish this." I gesture to the poor excuse of a father with his head lolled to the side, his severed fingers still in his mouth.

"No. I want this," he says, surprising the hell out of me.

He used to leave before partaking in the dirty work. He grabs our father's head by his hair and angles his head up straight.

"It was always going to come to this moment right here. You ruined our lives and so many others. Have fun in hell, Pop."

My eyes go wide as he takes a letter opener that lies on top of a stack of forgotten papers before plunging it into the side of our father's neck. Marco removes it, then plunges it back in. Again and again. I finally grab his arm once our father is long since dead and his neck mangled to a pulp.

Marco went into a trance as he repeatedly stabbed him. He was panting, shaking, and whispering unintelligible words.

It's then I realize he might have had it just as hard, or harder, than I did, which is fucking with me since our father doted on him. He was the golden son. But was he? Or was he just another one of my father's victims?

"I'll call this in. Why don't you go get cleaned up?" I say, looking at his shirt and slacks, red splatter covering his entire front.

He nods his head as he walks to the door. He hesitates before looking back at me.

"I'm sorry." Those are his only departing words before he leaves me with the dead pile of shit.

I sit on my father's dark leather sofa and light a blunt. I need serenity to replace my anxious elation. Even though I feel a weight lift as I take in my father's lifeless form, another sits with more pressure at the prospect of something worse waiting to take us out.

My thumb hovers over Alexa's father's number, but I hesitate, deciding to check Alexa's location instead, as I do several times a day. The necklace was a special gift but also included a tracker. As long as she keeps it on, I have peace of mind, to an extent.

After everything Marco informed us of, it seems the necklace was fitting. As was the anklet I gave Rosie as a wedding gift, which also carries a tracker that Vic monitors.

The only time either of the trackers don't work are in Alexa's place, thanks to her not-so-stupid friend.

Trey asked for Jenna's details, and I gave him what I had to offer, which was limited. I'm glad she caught his eye. Now he can do some of the work and report back to me with his findings. Something isn't right. She doesn't exist from what I'm able to find. It's like she fell from the sky or some shit.

Alexa's currently at home since I'm unable to see her. I day-dream about what she's doing. Probably cursing me to the pits of hell.

I've been racking my brain at what I can do to get her to come around. At some point, she will need to help me run everything. Especially her father's legacy, which I know she cares about deeply, but refuses to do so with me by her side.

I linger over the candid wedding photos I took, her unaware-ness making them even more precious. She's breathtakingly beautiful. I tried to persuade her to come home with me last night, with no success.

My finger hovers over her father's number. I need to inform him and the rest of the heads about the findings. I will not keep them in the dark like my father did. That's not how I want to roll.

As a boss, I thrive off respect and honesty. How can I expect that of them if I don't give it in return?

Twenty

Alexa

I regard the small black box in my hands with trepidation. An innocent red bow sits at the top, but I'm sure there's nothing innocent in the box.

Another gift from Gage.

One he handed to me as I left Rosie's wedding last night.

I'm still in shock at how amazing everything turned out. And to think it was Gage who helped with all the festivities. I could almost kiss him for making Rosie so happy. Almost.

Each interaction with him is one unfortunate event after another. I've been attempting to play hard to get like a seasoned pro, but when he's near, it's like I can't stand on solid ground.

My legs turn to jelly, as if knowing he'll be there to sweep me up in his warm, muscular arms.

Some of it can be attributed to the familiarity and closeness we've always shared, but now there's an undeniable sexual chemistry that can't be ignored, even though I've tried.

When we were younger, it simmered just under the surface, a gentle, manageable boil. But this—this is different. It's consuming me.

And while I'm caught in the trap that is Gage himself, I don't want to get out. If anything, I want to be bound further to him. It's unsettling and dangerous to my heart.

Jenna captures my attention as she enters my room, her tired face drawing my gaze as she climbs into bed beside me. Dark circles cast shadows on her otherwise flawless porcelain skin, revealing restless nights. Her absence has become more frequent lately, which concerns me, especially coupled with how exhausted she's been.

"Someone left this by the door," Jenna says as she holds up another red rose. I swear they keep on popping up everywhere I go. What is it now? Number nine? Ten?

"Throw it away. I don't want it."

Now, knowing what I do, it's probably from Gage.

"I'll keep it for myself since no one buys me shit," she says as she smells it deeply.

The dark circles and bags are even more pronounced the closer she gets.

"You look exhausted. Up all night talking to your biker daddy?" I grin.

Jenna's nose scrunches in disgust. "I'm with Rosie. That name is awful."

"Only when it's directed at you."

"Nothing is going on between him and me."

"Yeah, sure, it looked like it from the way he was tracking you all night like you were his last supper on death row."

"You're imagining things. What's that?" Jenna points at Gage's gift I have yet to open.

"More lies," I state before throwing the box haphazardly on my nightstand with a thunk.

"Sounds fun. Give it here."

"Nope. It's staying closed until I'm ready."

"What if it's your engagement ring?"

My eyes widen in horror. "Then it's definitely staying in there."

"The anticipation might kill me," Jenna whines.

"I'll play all your favorite songs at your funeral."

She grins. "Promise?"

I give a noncommittal shrug. Jenna smiles before jumping over me like a ninja. She grabs the box and opens it like a child on Christmas morning before I can comment further.

She chuckles. "How very early 2000s Mafia Daddy. I wonder if this even works."

That has me jumping from my bed with speed I didn't know I could muster so early in the morning. "Give it here, and I think I'm with you on the daddy talk."

"Nah, his nickname has a ring to it." Jenna grins as she studies the small iPod in her hands. "What do you think's on here? A sex track for your wedding night?" Her eyebrows wiggle.

"I swear your mind is always in the gutter. Must be your little friend with the creepy eyes making you all hot and bothered."

Jenna pauses before forcing her face into a neutral, emotionless mask. Every time I bring up the guy I now know as Trey, she acts strange. If she likes the guy, she should go for it, as I've told her multiple times. She's been tight-lipped about anything to do with him.

Jenna opens her mouth to say something witty, I'm sure, but I use that as my moment to rip the iPod out of her hands.

She grumbles, "My reflexes are shit this morning. I'm going to go crash out. When you listen to it, let me know. I'm dying to know how cheesy Mafia Daddy really is."

With that, she walks out, and I'm again left with my thoughts.

I can't help but smile as I look down at the small, worn iPod, a relic from my past. I flip it over and run my thumb over Gage's engraved initials on the back. As teens, we would make each other playlists. Music was something we both bonded over.

We passed the iPod between us more times than I could count, creating hundreds of playlists. This device is featherlight, yet it's heavy in my hands.

Nostalgia washes over me as vivid recollections of our joyful laughter and carefree days surge through me, igniting a roller coaster of emotions while I lovingly caress the initials one last time, my eyes welling up with tears.

A heavy sigh escapes my lips as I reach for the box, my fingers brushing against a folded piece of black paper tucked inside. I reach for it, but then I hesitate. I feel like I'm not ready to read whatever is on this note, so I carefully put the iPod back into the box and close it.

My phone dings with a notification, and I know it's him without checking. He sends me a million text messages a day, and if not that, he will call relentlessly.

Sometimes I answer. Most of the time I don't.

The Liar

> Meet me at our house in 30.

Alexa

> Our house? There is no "our"!

The Liar

> What's mine is yours, and what's yours is mine, baby.

Alexa

> Gag

The Liar

> You gagging on my cock sounds lovely. Meet me at our house or I'm coming to your condo. Maybe we'll go for round two? I distinctly remember you loving what I did the last time I was there.

I gulp at the reminder of being tied and spanked with a gag in my mouth. That's something I can never forget. Nor would I ever want to, much to my dismay.

The Liar

> 27 minutes. You're wasting time.

What a persistent, controlling dick. I'm tempted to stand his ass up just to show him who's in charge. But nothing has gone according to plan when I go against him.

Alexa

> I'll see you in an hour and not one minute before.

The Liar

> I'll be counting down the minutes.

Ugh. I throw my phone on the bed. He's so infuriating.

I rush through getting ready because I wouldn't put it past him to still show up. I'll be in his territory at his house, but I can't have him in mine after that tainted night. Jenna also has a key, and I guarantee she would find me in a compromising position, and I'd never live that shit down.

I follow my GPS to a row of black-and-white townhomes that stand alarmingly close to my condo... like, mere minutes.

The dick was right under my nose the whole time, and I was oblivious. It's a damn good thing my future job isn't as a private investigator because I'd suck.

I confidently stride through his front door without bothering to knock, a small act of rebellion mirroring his own uninvited entrance into my domain.

I'm greeted by a sparse, almost clinically clean space. It looks like a model home. Complete with beautiful paintings and a modern black, white, and tan color scheme. The distinct scent of his infuriatingly delicious cologne and marijuana permeate the air as I enter, leaving no doubt that I'm in his home.

"Gage?" I call out as I walk through the lower level. Where the hell is he?

I walk up the stairs to the second-floor landing. As I pass countless closed doors, I reach one at the end that is illuminated with bright lights.

To the left, an enormous black canopy platform bed and oversized furniture dominate the space.

As I walk in, the sound of running water fills the room. I continue to walk and peek around the corner to the right, where a bathroom sits.

Billowing steam fills the shower, obscuring my vision, but I can still make out Gage through the hazy air. His back, kissed by the sun and adorned with tattoos, is a sight to behold. With each movement, his muscles flex as he uses his firm hands to scrub his scalp with shampoo.

His special scent of darkness and spice lingers in the bathroom, enticing me to take an involuntary step closer.

I lick my dry lips as the inevitable hunger and longing that's now associated with Gage runs through my body.

He soaps up his body while I watch the suds run down his muscular ass and equally muscular legs, which are also covered in ink. He is perfection, and I, unfortunately and undoubtedly, can't take my eyes off him, even if I wanted to.

The longer I stand here and watch him, the hotter I feel. My skin is burning and blushing with a strange, feverish warmth. I should leave. This isn't right. I'm a total creep for watching him without his knowledge, but it's just like at his club, in those rooms. I'm unable to avert my gaze. He continues to wash himself, and by some miracle, I snap out of my haze.

I attempt to take a step back just as Gage faces me. The water from the showerhead beads off his skin.

His eyes pin me in place as a mischievous smirk adorns his face. He licks his full lips before holding his full bottom lip prisoner with his teeth.

With a crook of his long, tattooed finger, he beckons me closer, his eyes full of sin. I take a deep gulp, my throat tightening, before vigorously shaking my head in refusal.

Despite my desire to retreat now that I'm caught, I find myself rooted to the spot as he persistently gestures for me to come closer. My eyes widen as he decides for me.

Gage is dripping wet, soap still running trails down his hard body as he steps forward and out of his walk-in shower. I try my best to keep my eyes above the waist. It's a task that requires more effort than I ever imagined, and I might have accidentally peeked because... wow.

His front presses against mine, and his nose runs up and down my neck before he groans into my ear.

I take a deep breath in as goose bumps form like a fever all over my body.

My hands move to his wet back as I hold on to him.

"I missed you." Gage's deep, breathy voice reverberates through the bathroom.

"I..." *Can't form a sentence.*

I lick my parched lips again, which now resemble the aridity of a desert.

Gage chuckles at my state. "Shower with me."

I shake my head again since words evade me. He takes a step back with me still glued to him, and I gaze up into his deep blue ocean-colored eyes. They're burning into me, so much so that I have to avert my gaze, but what has me pausing are the red dots against his neck.

"What's that?" I grab his jaw with my thumb and forefinger and turn his head to the side, revealing more red dots. No, not dots, blood. "Are you hurt?"

Gage's body grows tense against me for a fraction of a second, making my stomach drop.

"I killed my father this morning."

A gasp escapes my lips.

"I'm telling you this because you're about to become a boss, but I'd like it if you'd keep it from Rosie."

"And what about Marco? Does he know?"

Gage's eyes narrow at my mention of his brother. "He helped... and Vic."

As I stand there, his words hang in the air, slowly sinking in, causing shock to wash over me. I've always been able to look past what my dad does to a certain extent. In my mind, he has two lives and never lets them mingle. He never lets his dark side taint the wonderful life we have. It provided a sense of security for my mom and me. It kept us believing he was the most amazing man to walk the planet.

But now I have to walk into the dark with Gage by my side, hand in hand, and I'm still trying to come to terms with that.

Their father wasn't a good man. He was all the bad parts of this life and brought nothing light home. Rosie could not move past the knowledge of what he did; it devastated her.

However, I swiftly digested and released it, refusing to let it weigh me down. It was because of that my dad knew I'd be able to lead. Little did he know I'd fuck it up later and not be able to perform when I needed to the most. The thought often crossed my mind, and still does, questioning whether my dad would be happier if he had a son instead of me. I know he loves me, but I know a son leading would appear more powerful.

I snap out of my dark musings as Gage waves his hand in front of my face, where I see another drop of dried blood.

"Un-fucking-believable!" I say, taking a large step back and out of his arms. My eyebrows scrunch as I point a finger at him. "You just killed your father, his blood still stains your skin, and you want to have sex? What the fuck is wrong with you?"

As his lips quirk into a smirk, I shake my head and my gaze unfortunately takes more of him in, including his very hard cock. The talk of murder is turning him on.

What the fucking fuck?

I take another step in retreat; one he takes as a challenge as he follows my step.

"Make no mistake, his rotting corpse can be lying on the bed, and I'd still fuck you right next to him."

"You're sick!"

"Never said I was well, baby."

Jesus, I'm going to marry a fucking psycho with a killing fetish.

He extends his hand out to me. "Now come shower with me."

"Not a chance in hell, you freaking psycho! Wash your sins off and meet me downstairs. Maybe I'll still be here, maybe not." I shrug.

"If you run, I'll chase you, and we both know how much my *piccolo angello* likes that." His atrocious nickname throws me off as he flashes me a wicked smile, which makes my pulse jump and my core flutter.

My brain needs to have a serious talk with my body.

"Fuck you!" I flip him off. His laughter mixes with my loud steps as I stomp down the hallway.

Twenty-One

Gage

D escending the stairs, I quirk a brow as the aroma of eggs and bacon fills the air.

My steps are measured as I come around the corner and see Alexa. One of her delicate hands confidently wields a spatula, while the other casually rests on her white apron-draped hip as the sound of food sizzles.

Where the hell did she find an apron, and is she wearing one of my black shirts?

I lean against the wall, watching as she rifles through the drawers, the wood creaking softly under her touch. Totally unaware of my gaze, she absentmindedly blows on a lock of dark brown hair that escaped her messy bun resting on the crown of her head. She's never been more beautiful than right now. To have her in our house is a sight I've always dreamed of and longed for.

I yearn to trail behind her, my arms encircling her waist, while I plant kisses on her neck. And more, I want her to lean back against me with her head on my chest and a smile on her face.

I shift to more of a standing position as she gazes up at me.

"Don't stop on my account. Looks like you made yourself right at home."

"What's yours is mine, and what's mine is yours," she mocks.

"I'm glad you're finally conceding to your reality."

She scoffs. "Like fuck I am. I was hungry."

Observing the island, I see she not only made herself a plate but also prepared one for me. She remembered my dislike for runny egg yolk, so she scrambled them instead of cooking them sunny side up like the other plate. A smirk plays on my lips as I meet her gaze again. Instantly, her eyes narrow with suspicion.

"And I see you're already doing your wifely duties."

"I'm an equal. Not a fucking maid, servant, or secretary made just for you."

"I'm kidding. You know I see you as more than that. You're my partner. My other half."

Her head drops to the counter. "We're here to discuss different matters."

"They're interconnected. We should discuss everything."

"Oh, goody."

"I'm not the worst choice for a husband."

"Could have fooled me."

I cross my arms over my chest in defense. "What makes me so awful?"

As she brings her hand up, I brace myself for what's coming, knowing she's about to tally my mistakes. Her middle finger comes up first.

"You lied about your identity."

"That was—"

"I'm not done. The cameras were a huge invasion of my privacy, and you breaking into my place at night was unacceptable."

"All things you enjoyed."

"Still not done." She bites her lip and looks anywhere but at me before continuing. "My virginity."

I regard her with confusion. "What about it?"

"You took it, dick, and it wasn't memorable in a good way whatsoever."

"You mean..."

"Yep. My first time was awful. Thanks."

"It was my first, too."

"Your first what?" She quirks a brow.

"My first time."

"I don't want to hear *all your lies*, Gage. They won't make me feel any better."

"I'm not," I say as I blow out a breath. I think back to Halloween and grimace as I think of the way I thrusted into her so ruthlessly. It probably hurt like a motherfucker. "I'm so sorry, I—"

"You know, it's kind of hard to believe, considering you own a sex club."

"The club isn't what you think."

"So you're saying it's not a sex club? Could have fooled me with all the, I don't know, sex rooms."

"It is, but I built it with reasons..."

"I'm not following."

I sigh. This isn't what I wanted to talk about with her today.

"My father brought me to the Stockade for years. I watched his men bring young women in under the guise of a fun time after they had one too many drinks at a bar or club. They were into it until they weren't. Until they understood there were only two ways they would leave: in a bag or as someone's property. I burned the Stockade down because of what it represented, but I still understood the necessity of providing a place for like-minded people to come and explore their desires in a safe, consensual space."

She eyes me suspiciously. "And where do you fit into all of this? What's the sex club for you?"

"I like the money, and I'm fascinated by control. Maybe because I had none."

I stop at that. Though those are important, my primary reason was to ensure I could meet her needs and desires, both physically and emotionally, without her realizing my insecurities since I was so inexperienced. I wanted her to crave my touch. To lean into my dominating presence while begging me for more.

"Well, I'm sure you could achieve that in other ways."

"I..." My gaze shifts for a moment. I need to get my shit under control. My patience is slipping, and the need to lay everything out, bare, including my heart, is taking precedence over the rejection I will most likely receive because of how epically I've fucked this up.

I take a deep breath. Fuck it, I'll talk to her through not only these eyes but the eyes of the boy who was her friend first.

I hold her stare as she regards me with confusion in her eyes. "I've wanted you since we were young. All the best memories have been with you by my side. At first, it was innocent. Your presence alone made me happy. You made everything feel like Christmas morning. I'd go to sleep at night with a smile on my face, knowing I'd see you the following morning. Then, it turned into something deeper. The way you looked, your sweet coconut smell, your laugh, your smile, your witty, smart-ass personality were addictive, and it no longer became just Christmas morning. It was the Fourth of July when I hugged you, fireworks shooting through my body in vivid colors. It was New Year's Eve when we sat and listened to music together in the dark, so achingly close. A party for us, and us alone. No alcohol was necessary for the intoxicating effect you had on me. You have and will always be everything I've ever wanted, ever needed. I want you to have the same feelings for me as I have for you. I want you to want me, and I was worried I wouldn't be enough."

A tear escapes the confines of her lid and slowly descends her cheek. Alexa has always been strong, so the tear she sheds isn't taken lightly.

"Gage. I-I," she stutters, and it kills me.

"Don't say anything. I just—I just wanted to tell you," I say, anxiously running my hand against my scalp. The idea of her rejecting me after I confessed my feelings is agonizing.

"But—"

"Don't," I plead.

She looks at me for a beat, her eyes lingering before dropping back to the counter; a nervous cough escapes her throat. "I appreciate your honesty. Something you haven't given me since making your grand appearance back into my life. You know, if you had told me it was you from the start, things between us would be different."

"Would we be as close as we are now, or would we be in the same place as we were before I left for prison?"

"I don't know—"

"Exactly. Maybe I should have gone about it differently—"

"You think?" She mutters.

"But," When she gives me a dirty look, I decide to stop while I'm ahead. This conversation will get us nowhere. What's done is done. "All this is irrelevant now. I was your first kiss and your first time, and we're getting married. That's all that matters."

"Marco was my first kiss."

My body tenses. "When?"

"A party in college," she says with a dismissive shrug.

"What party?"

"A costume party."

"The angel and devil one?" I ask.

"How did you...?" Her mind works over that night. "You—"

"You looked beautiful that night in the garden."

"How long have you been watching me?"

"Since I got out."

"And you never thought to, I don't know, just show yourself or write me back even once?" she asks as her hand lands on her hip.

"There were things that needed to be taken care of first. I needed to weaken my father's power and influence."

What she doesn't know is I wanted to believe I deserved her, and I thought those actions would make me believe it, but they didn't, and I don't know if they ever will.

"Bullshit, Gage. Do you have any idea the hole that was left when you went away? How I cried myself to sleep night after night, or how I prayed that you'd write me back, but you never did? My heart broke into a million pieces. I felt abandoned by you. You hurt me, and you never came back to fix it once you were free. You disappeared." Tears rim her eyes once more.

A sharp pain pierces my chest as I listened to her account of how my departure affected her. I knew she'd be upset, but I didn't think it ran that deep. Am I enough of an asshole to find comfort in knowing my absence hurt her just as much as it hurt me? Yes, yes, I am.

"I'm sorry. I didn't think you'd be that upset."

As I walk around the kitchen island, the need to hold her and make a promise to never leave her side again rages through me. I want her to know that I'm here forever.

"Don't even think about it. We haven't finished."

I stop mid-stride and put my hands up in surrender.

"What else do I need to know? Everything needs to come out in the open right now, or you lose me forever."

"After I got out, I started following Marco, my father, and a few other people within the families."

"So I wasn't the only lucky one?"

"That fucking mouth. It makes me want to bend you over my knee and spank the living shit out of you."

She scrunches her nose. "I'd like to see you try. I wasn't ready last time."

"I think you weren't ready on purpose."

"And I think you're delusional. Now stop changing the subject."

"I started following people and making connections, like with Vic's MC. My father's ledgers had a lot of inconsistencies, and they were connected to the MC. Most were just conjecture until this morning. To make a long-ass story short, my father paid an assassin or hitman group to take out members of the families. He even attempted to have Rosie kidnapped at one point, but the details are pretty hazy, and I need to find out more. He also put a hit out on your father."

Her face pales. "What?"

"Marco found out and shut it down, so don't worry."

"That's why you killed him?"

"That, among many other reasons." I leave it vague. She doesn't need to know the ugliness associated with my father and his office of horrors my brother and I faced. There are a few reasons I have tattoos covering most of my body. Scars from my father's sadistic lessons being one of them.

"What happens now?" Alexa says with a frown.

"It's time to bring our families together, but if you'd like, we can consummate said marriage right now. Let me make up for the last time."

"You're unbelievable, you know that."

"Have dinner with me tonight."

She sighs. "It's never as simple as just dinner with you."

"Just give me a chance." She silently stares at me. "Please."

"We aren't having dinner at your club."

"Our club."

"Be serious for once," she grumbles.

"Fine. We'll go somewhere else. Happy?"

"No."

"I'll pick you up at six."

"I'll drive myself."

"Cut the bullshit. The only reason girls do that is if they don't trust the guy they're having dinner with."

"Exactly." She smirks.

"Your dramatics are both tiring and unwarranted."

Twenty-Two

Alexa

My doorbell rings precisely at six. I already know who it is. I open the door and gaze into Gage's deep-blue eyes.

This is our first official date, though I'd never tell him I thought of it as such. It would go right to his head.

His black suit molds to his body, conveying power and control—not just physically, but mentally, and perhaps spiritually, as the effect he has on me when I'm near him would suggest.

I step out and lock the door, and when I turn around, we're almost chest to chest, which makes my body hum with awareness.

Then, he holds up a rose and I remember why I'm so irritated with him and his lies and why I still need to keep these feelings locked up tight.

"I don't want that."

"Neither do I. Who the fuck is putting roses on your porch?"

I raise a brow. "Don't act like you haven't been doing it. Your silly little game is over."

"I haven't put anything on your porch besides those gift boxes."

"You sure?"

"I remember you saying cutting a rose from the bush where it was born was like killing it."

My head tilts as I regard him. "You remember that? I said that forever ago."

"I remember everything. Now, who?"

"I-I don't know," I say, my voice wavering as I take a deep, shaky breath. The thought of Gage leaving roses pissed me off because that meant he was following my every move. But now I'm creeped out because someone I don't know is following me. "It started weeks ago."

"Just here?"

"No, on my car or Jenna's when we would be out together," I say as I bite my lip. "But it could be someone bothering her. She works as a bartender at a strip club. I'll ask her about it."

Gage looks around. He has a white-knuckle grip on the rose stem.

"I thought we were going out to eat," I say, hoping to derail whatever murderous plot he has running through his head.

He glances back at me with a huge grin before grabbing my hand. "Then let's go."

The car ride is silent aside from the low music in the background. I steal a glance at Gage as he drives, obviously lost in thought.

Something is intriguing about his nose—a slight upturn at the tip, contrasting with a subtle bump on the bridge that suggests a history of many injuries. His lips are fuller than I recall, and I can confirm they possess a softness matching their appearance. His beard has grown in the past few days, giving him a more rugged appearance, which contrasts with his polished suit. My attention shifts to his firm grip on the steering wheel. Even through his tattoos, the bulging veins in his hand are visible. I lick my extremely dry lips and blow out a breath.

"Like what you see?"

"What?" I murmur as I lift my gaze.

He keeps his eyes on the road, but his grin is huge.

"You heard me."

"I don't know what you're talking about," I say, averting my eyes to the road ahead.

"Yeah, sure."

"Whatever." I move my hand to the volume of the radio and turn it up loud enough to drown out his laughter.

The moment I hear the beginning beat, my head whips to him. "This song is so old. I haven't heard it in forever." One song drowns into the next, all old and from our teens. "You know, there are new songs out there."

Gage stays quiet for a minute before his eyes reach mine. "When I went in, time stood still for a while. These songs represent good memories, and I guess I've held onto them. Don't get me wrong, I got to listen to music in there, but the new stuff is complete shit and doesn't hit the same."

My heart aches as I hear his words. I've been so lost in the bitter taste of his betrayal that I overlooked the long years his life was at a standstill. He missed out on so much and will never get that time back.

Before I know it, we pull up to the valet of a restaurant I've never been to. I step out, and Gage rests his hand on the small of my back as we walk through the front doors. It isn't lost on me how good his hand feels as he guides me to a secluded circular booth far into the restaurant.

As I scoot in, I survey my surroundings. The inside of the restaurant is dark and moody. Not like at the club, but dark in a Victorian Gothic aesthetic. Intricate pointed arches are at every booth entrance. Each arch has delicate carvings. Black is the most prevalent color on the walls, floors, booths, and tables. A gold chandelier sits high over our table with dozens of real candles to light our meal.

"Wow. This place is beautiful."

"Just like you," Gage whispers in my ear.

My head snaps his way as I lean back. "Why are you so close?"

His only answer is a smirk as he leans closer to me.

"Good evening, Mr. Moretti and..." I straighten as I gaze at a server in his mid-fifties.

"Mrs. Moretti." My head whips back to Gage as his hand rests on my thigh and gives it a little squeeze, halting my objection.

"Oh, my apologies. Congratulations, sir."

"Thank you," Gage says with a huge smile even though I'm shooting him daggers with my eyes and failing to wrench his hand from my lap.

"What can I get for you tonight?"

"We will have the three course. All sauces on the side, please."

"Right away, sir," the server says before bowing and walking away.

"Why did you order for me? What if I don't like it?"

"Steak because it's your favorite. Sauces on the side since you're weird about them."

"You're... intense," I say, at a loss for words.

I wonder if it will always be like this, with him taking the lead at every turn. I'm uncertain whether I despise it, or worse, enjoy it.

"You smell good."

"Thanks," I say as I try to scoot away from him.

His grip locks on my thigh. "Why do you have to make everything so fucking difficult? Just sit next to me, please."

"We thought that was you." I glance up and see Mr. Gualtieri and Mr. Baccalieri, two of my father's three associates.

Like my dad, they're also retiring. It's a weird tradition. There are five families, Moretti being the boss at the top of the pyramid, Rossi, Gualtieri, Baccalieri, and Lombardi being the respective capos. When the last heir becomes of age at twenty, a transition of power takes place. The parents retire and make way for the younger generation to step up, which is us. There is no ambiguity in the rules; they are straightforward and nonnegotiable. We must have arranged marriages between the families for strength and alliance, and we must have children simultaneously, ensuring our offspring grow up together and form a bond. We then relinquish control and let them lead the way.

Usually, you hear about a head dying and someone taking over, but not in our pillar of the Italian Mafia. Its intention is to maintain peace by discouraging individuals from engaging in a power-hungry struggle for wealth and influence.

The thought of Gage and me having to uphold said tradition has me glancing over at him with trepidation. Children will be expected, and soon. I don't know how I feel about that. Though I've always dreamed of having a large, loving family. And I'm sure Gage would be a wonderful, nurturing father, just like my dad.

"It's nice to see you, gentlemen," Gage says as he stands to shake their hands. "I spoke with Manuel, Tony, and Rocco today. Everything's looking good."

The thought of their sons makes me wince. With no rules to govern their actions as children, chaos and destruction became their primary interests whenever we all got together. From them lighting my playhouse on fire to taking my dad's Maclaren on a joyride—and I'm sure that's not even the worst of it.

Since I last saw them, I doubt they've transformed into anything other than monstrous beings. It's going to be painful working in such proximity, especially since Gage, Marco, Rosie, and I never bonded with them like we were supposed to. The clash of power and dominance was always present, making it clear they considered themselves superior. However, Gage and Marco will always be superior and rein over them. It's just the way it is and will always be.

"Yes, we heard about the fat that was trimmed. I had my doubts, but I think you'll be a fine leader," Mr. Gualtieri mutters. It takes a minute to realize the fat he's talking about is Gage's father. Gross.

"It serves as a reminder to those who cross me, blood or not," Gage says with a hard edge. The warning's clear in his words. He doesn't give a fuck who you are. He will take you down if need be.

They say goodbye to Gage and take their leave without even acknowledging my presence. They are one of many who aren't happy about me taking my dad's position. The thought leaves me with a mix of anxiety and irritation.

"I'm not looking forward to working with their sons."

"You have nothing to worry about," Gage says with a confidence I wished I possessed.

I bump my shoulder against his with a small grin. "Do you remember giving Tony a black eye for trying to cut my hair?"

His eyes light up. "How can I forget? He was shocked as hell when I tackled him. They always thought I was a pushover because I was quiet. It was nice to finally reveal a piece of my true self."

"Is this your true self?" I ask as I gesture at him.

"What do you mean?"

"You're dark, demanding, and kind of crazy."

He grins but ignores my assessment of him.

"You'll get the respect you deserve. I won't tolerate anything less."

I wish I shared his optimism.

"What if I can't... do it?" I whisper. "The hard stuff."

Gage's eyes soften as he looks at me. His eyes drift to my hand in my lap, and he puts his hand on top of mine before lacing our fingers together and gazing back up at me. It's strange. I've never been overly fond of touch. I'm more of an acts of service type, but I can't deny the way his touch has always comforted me in the way my body needs.

"We are one, Lex. I'm your safe place, and you are mine. We strengthen each other, and together, there is nothing we can't do."

With each word he speaks, and the conviction in his eyes, my doubts fade away, and my heart races in response.

He squeezes my hand, his touch firm and reassuring, before gently pressing his forehead against mine. The moment our skin touches, the clatter of plates and murmur of conversations in the restaurant fades into blissful silence. All that remains is Gage's warm skin, his intense eyes, and our lips a whisper length apart.

I'm torn, as I always am with him. If I initiate this, if I lean in and touch his lips to mine, there's no going back. This will be me forgiving and forgetting.

Gage's phone rings, and we both break apart.

"Fuck," Gage mutters as he answers his phone.

His face twists from a slight frown of irritation into a mask of furious rage in mere seconds.

"I'm on my way." He gazes at me with regret. "We have to go."

"Why?"

"Problem at the club."

"Me getting interrupted at a restaurant is becoming a regular thing. I don't like it," I say as he grabs my hand and pulls me out of the booth. "Don't we need to tell them or pay? I'm sure they made some of the food."

"They'll put it on my tab," he says as we make our way to the entrance.

"So you have a habit of bringing dates here?" I say with displeasure in my tone and my heart heavy at the thought. I try for sarcastic and pissy, but I'm sure the jealousy clearly shows.

"We own the restaurant, and I've never been on a date besides with you. But I love how jealous you are at the thought of another girl with me. Careful, Lex. You're starting to show you really care." He closes my car door with a smirk.

Twenty-Three

Gage

We make it to the club in record time, the bass from the music pulsating through the air. The club has never experienced an incident until now. My security urgently informed me of a member who's forcefully holding a partner against their will in one of the themed rooms.

The club operates under a strict set of policies. You fuck up once, and you're out for life. As adults, we know the difference between right and wrong. Some need liquid courage before a scene to loosen up. I have a one-drink max for anyone going into a themed room, Wanderland, or any of the other attractions we offer.

Every member is aware of the eyes on them to protect their safety. Listening devices are in rooms in case we have someone who decides not to follow our rules.

This one has broken three rules so far and has now barricaded himself in the room with his partner.

With Alexa remaining in my office, I proceed to the medical examination room.

I go to the false panel and click it open. They were first made for my comfort, but also for reasons such as this. The member placed a chair and desk against the door, but it is now rendered a useless attempt as I walk in through the hidden passage.

The moment I step inside, the sound of sniffling fills the air. I notice a woman with short blond hair sitting in the corner, with a man hovering over her.

Just as the secret door clicks shut, the man abruptly turns to face me.

"Get the fuck out!"

The camera lens, positioned in the far corner of the room, catches my gaze. With a frustrated sigh, I signal for the feed to end. The red light dims to black as I stalk toward the man.

I slowly roll my dress-shirt sleeves to my elbows with a tightness in my chest as the rage inside me rises. My patience runs thin with most, but violence inflicted upon women is high on the list.

I gaze over his lengthy, slender body that appears to have never lifted a weight. Then, recognition hits. It's that fucker who took Alexa out. I can still see fine bruising around his neck from when I practically strangled the life out of him. Seems like a mistake was made and I should have finished the job the other night.

"You," he mutters as he realizes who he just pissed off.

With each step I take forward, he retreats, edging closer to the woman, which compels me to come to a halt. His gaze shifts from her to me.

"We still have another hour in this room. You can have the lying bitch when I'm done."

With my temper barely contained, my hands ball into fists at my sides.

"I made my rules simple for stupid fucks like yourself, and you still broke them. Your membership is revoked. You need to leave now."

"And who the fuck are you?"

"The owner. Get the fuck out before I physically remove you myself."

"That bitch played hard to get with me because she was here, fucking the owner every weekend. Fucking figures," he snorts.

When he brings up Alexa, a red hue fills my vision. His eyes widen as I tackle him to the ground. With each strike, the sound of my fists connecting with his face echoes in the room. The sight of blood splattering on my knuckles is like a comforting lost friend, blurring the line between his pain and my pleasure. He lies there unconscious as I'm pulled off him by a couple of my security guards who broke the door down.

My gaze swings to Jace. "Take care of her. Make sure she has no injuries and give her whatever she needs."

Jace steps in front of the woman, who's huddled in the corner with her head pressed against the wall. She quivers in fear and tries to scurry away, but he provides comfort by caressing her back and whispering into her ear. As he picks her up, her arms wrap around his neck, and they leave the room.

"Drop him off at the hospital," I tell one of my security as I observe the stupid fuck's chest, barely rising and falling. "He's lucky he isn't dead."

I make my way to a storage room adjacent to my office, which conveniently includes a bathroom and is stocked with spare clothes. I take a quick shower and make myself presentable.

Alexa doesn't need to know about this. She has enough on her mind. I can't believe she's scared that she doesn't have what it takes to be the boss her father was. What she doesn't understand is that she has all that and more. She's the perfect mix of her father and her mother. Strong, loyal, and witty. She just needs to find the confidence, and I'm going to help her do it. Alexa's ascent to becoming one of the first female bosses fills me with immense pride.

I walk into my office and find her sitting behind my desk. She looks good there.

"Everything okay?" she asks as she looks me up and down. "You changed shirts."

"Mine was dirty from the food."

"We never ate, dick. Don't lie to me."

"Well, let's fix that. I'll see that Four Senses is open for us to dine."

"With the lights on."

"Are you sure?" I ask with a mischievous smirk.

We sit in Four Senses ten minutes later with the lights on, to my disappointment. Alexa looks around with a smile.

"This place is beautiful. You should let people dine with the lights on."

"Most prefer them to be off," I mutter.

Her cheeks blush a delightful shade of red as she clears her throat and looks anywhere but at me. "The date on my necklace is in fifteen days."

I nod. "It is."

"Nothing's been planned—"

"I saw to most of the planning since you haven't exactly been agreeable." I grin, even though her refusal of our upcoming wedding has hurt like a motherfucker.

"Shouldn't I be in charge, considering it's my wedding?"

A wave of relief washes over me at the thought of her finally taking our future seriously, of her finally taking me seriously.

"You always said you wanted a small wedding. Never wanting to be the center of attention. You'd rather have a lengthy honeymoon, which I'm definitely looking forward to," I say as I lick my lips.

"I want to backpack through Europe. Visit medieval castles and run through rolling hills of tulip fields, hence the lengthy honeymoon. Get your mind out of the gutter."

"Fine. We'll get married at my parents' house, in Mom's rose garden, as you once said you wanted... unless that's changed?"

"What about...?" She moves her hands around, attempting to find words before whispering, "The fat that was trimmed, or whatever Mr. Gualtieri said."

"The house was cleaned, if that's what you're worried about."

"It won't bother you to be there?"

"Not in the least."

"Okay," she says with a whimsical smile. "I loved being in that garden when I was younger."

"How could I forget? The dancing, the screaming..."

"You watched?"

"I watched you a lot."

"So you've been stalking me your whole life?"

"Something like that."

"That's pretty creepy, Gage."

I lean forward, across the table, which now seems too large and creates too much space between Alexa and me.

"I don't think you mind it."

She licks her lips before looking down at her half-eaten plate.

"And what about all the other details?" she asks.

"They don't matter right now. I want to show you another part of the club."

"I don't know if that's a good idea," she says, shaking her head.

"You were always so curious when we were younger. What happened to that girl?"

"She now has a sense of self-preservation." She shrugs.

"Or maybe she's just a chickenshit these days," I say with a smile.

"If I remember correctly, you were the chickenshit back in the day, not me. Still scared of the dark, Gage?" she asks as she leans closer to me, over the table. Her breasts are close to spilling out in this position, and I want nothing more than to shove my cock between them. I gaze into her eyes, which are full of goading mischief.

Alexa's eyes widen in surprise when I stand and stalk toward her. Standing over her, I watch as her back sinks further into the comfort of the backrest. With a tender touch, I place my index finger under her chin and lift until her eyes lock with mine.

"I was only scared of the dark because I enjoyed playing in its endlessness so much. I was the darkness, and I was terrified of it touching your light." My eyes track her throat as she visibly swallows, which makes me smirk in satisfaction. "Now, I not only want to touch your light but make it obsidian."

In one swift motion, I slide behind her chair and smoothly pull it out, lifting her effortlessly to her feet. With no resistance, I escort her out of the dining room. My words have obviously hit a cord and render her speechless for once. I like it.

As she trails behind me, I rush to the supply room to fetch us complimentary bathing suits and robes that the club has available for members. I pass the garments to her and gesture toward the women's dressing rooms. Once she's in and the door's locked, I stride purposely to the men's dressing rooms around the corner, change into my trunks with lightning speed, and then walk back to hers. The last thing I want is for her to vacate the dressing room and not see me waiting for her.

As the door clicks open, I glance up from where I'm leaning against the opposite wall. Her delectable body is enveloped in the plush white robe that I can't wait to unwrap. As my eyes move upward to her face, I catch a glimpse of the delicate pink flush on her cheeks. Noticing her reaction to me enjoying the view of her body, I smirk, to which she rolls her eyes in exasperation.

Closing the distance between us in just two steps, I extend my hand to grasp hers, and she accepts it, much to my amazement. I intertwine our fingers as I steer her down the hall to our destination.

"Get in," I say as I stand in the middle of the pool, my bottom half submerged in the warm water. The moment we entered the room, I let her hand go and jumped in, allowing her to take in the simulation.

With trepidation, she looks around at the dark water that appears to have endless depths despite me standing chest deep. "I'm—"

"Scared?" I supply. "The only thing that'll bite you in here is me."

Her gaze shifts to the side, where a captivating thunderstorm simulation plays on a large screen, creating a hypnotic experience with mist swirling from the ceiling and a gentle fog rising from the pool's surface.

She stands there, the vibrant red of the bikini contrasting against her fair skin. The reality of seeing her in this far exceeded the limits of my imagination.

I wade toward her in the water, causing her to move forward.

"Okay, okay, I'm getting in." She takes tentative steps. "Oh, it feels good in here."

As I watch her walk around in the water, I can't help but lick my lips in anticipation. Her lips curve into a gentle smile, radiating warmth. Her hair, once sleek and smooth, now clings to her wet body and has a slight wave as the mist comes down around her.

I want to rush her, grab her, and have my way with her. However, my refined side yearns to witness her sheer enjoyment.

As I constructed the club, I knew this feature had to be incorporated. Whenever it rained, no matter what she was doing or wherever she was, Alexa would pause, tilt her face to the sky, and embrace the droplets with a smile on her lips and arms outstretched. When I was lonely and sad, that memory echoed through me, and I longed to relive it.

Facing away from me, she stretches her arms outward while her palms hover just above the water's surface.

She turns toward me, her smile lighting up the dark room and etching itself into my memory. "This is amazing, and probably my favorite part of the club."

"It's one of mine too."

"And what about the others?" she asks before shaking her head. "Never mind. I don't want to know."

"Your jealousy is adorable but unnecessary. As I've mentioned before, I've only been with you."

"You were away for a long time. It's hard to believe you'd wait all this time for me."

I exhale and take in the surroundings of the dark water. "Thoughts of you and revenge consumed my mind while I was in there. Then, I was free, and you were still all I could imagine. I've always wanted you so fucking bad, and that will never change."

"And now we're here."

"We are," I say as I approach her.

To create distance, she takes a few steps back. "Down, boy."

"What?"

"You know what. I know what that look means."

"What does it mean?" I question with a smirk as I continue to stalk toward her.

Water sloshing against my chest grows louder as I quicken my pace. She swiftly turns and places her arms in front of her as she dives beneath the water's surface. Right before she fades into the inky blackness of the water, I hastily follow her and seize her ankle before tugging her back toward me. As she reaches the surface, she sputters, expelling water from her mouth, and wipes away the wetness on her face.

"You dick! I could have drowned," she says as she tries to get out of my arms.

"You were on the swim team for a decade. Stop with the dramatics."

"Ugh, you drive me crazy."

"Ditto, baby," I whisper in her ear, eliciting a shudder from her.

I tighten my grip on her while my tongue traces a path from her collarbone to her ear. I savor the taste of her skin and the sensation of goose bumps that have risen. Her breath hitches, and a moan escapes as I suck on her skin harder. She reaches her hand behind her and grabs my head as an anchor. My lips continue their exploration, tracing a path of suction and tender kisses down her neck until I spin her around.

She gazes up at me. Her baby-blue eyes shimmer with curiosity and longing, creating an inferno under my skin. I reach out, and my hands find their way into her hair, tugging tightly as our lips collide in a fiery, intense kiss. As I lift her, her moans mingle with mine, filling the surrounding air.

My cock sits perfectly against her center and is barely held back by my thin swim shorts and the small triangle of material she wears.

I intensify the grinding against her center, eliciting another passionate moan that mingles with our kiss.

She breaks the kiss and fixes her gaze on me, searching for something in my eyes.

"I'm not ready for that," she whispers.

"That's fine. We don't have to do that."

She might not be ready for sex, but I can provide her with pleasure and make her feel special in numerous other ways.

With her forehead pressed against mine, I guide us to the edge of the pool. Her back collides with the tiled wall with a small thud as her hands tangle in my hair. She grabs the longer strands on top and gives them a firm tug. The pain sends waves of pleasure coursing through my body. I suck on her bottom lip as I reach into the water and pull the string on her bikini bottom and then the other side before ripping it from between her legs.

"Wait," she says as she pulls back.

As I tug my swim shorts down, I firmly grab the back of her head, redirecting her focus to my eyes rather than my movements. "I got you. I always got you."

I push my hard cock against her soft folds, ensuring my cock rubs her clit with each thrust. Her body trembles and quivers against mine as I move up and down. Her nails dig into my back as I pick up the pace. The once peaceful water now crashes against us, causing the perfect storm to accompany the thunder and lightning of the projected image on the walls.

As our breaths quicken as a tingling sensation surges through my body.

"Oh, Gage," she says breathlessly. I maintain my steady pace but almost falter at finally hearing her moan my name.

The fake storm and mist fade into oblivion as she unravels in my arms. Her trembling body, filled with ecstasy, pushes me to surrender to the powerful force of my orgasm, which consumes me.

As I catch my breath, I lean against her, feeling the steady rise and fall of her chest.

"That—"

"Don't. Not right now," I whisper against her neck. I'm worried she's going to call what just transpired between us a mistake when it was the exact opposite. It was perfection.

I pull away and tug my shorts back up before reaching over her head and grabbing her discarded bottoms and handing them to her. She looks anywhere but at me as she puts them on.

"What was college like?" I ask to make things less tense.

"Why?" She frowns.

"I never got to experience it, so I'm curious."

A pained expression crosses her face before it softens. "Right, I'm sorry," she murmurs as she pushes away from the wall and glides in the surrounding water. "I liked it for what it was. I was able to play make-believe and feel freedom as I've never felt before. Then everything got shitty. The freedom I once felt turned into more of a prison sentence." She winces over at me. "Sorry, not the right choice of words."

"It's okay."

"It all just became so disappointing. Marco had a lot to do with that. And I think—no, I know, if you would have been there with us, the outcome would have been different."

"How so?"

"You were always the protector, the listener, the fixer. Rosie might not have left if you had been there. Although I'm happy she found love in the chaos," she says with a smile. "I never thanked you for that."

"You just did."

"What's the first thing you did when you got out?" she asks as she flips to her back and lets the water take her.

My smile broadens as I observe her. "You really want to know?"

"Now I'm not so sure."

"After having the best lobster of my life, I snuck into your room while you were sleeping."

Her eyes narrow at me as she stops floating. "I'd say I'm surprised, but I'm not. You're lucky my dad didn't kill you."

"I couldn't resist, especially since both he and your mom were conveniently out of town."

"And what did you do?"

"I sat and watched you for hours."

"You should have woken me up."

"Believe me, I thought about it," I say with a smirk. As I sat at the foot of her bed in her parents' house, I fantasized about tying her up, spanking her, and fucking her senseless. I didn't dare touch her that first night I snuck in. My patience was thin, and I knew one touch would've fucked all my planning to hell.

"There's that look again," she says, stepping back.

A laugh escapes me unexpectedly, and it sounds like it's from a different life, my old life. I miss this. I miss us.

She yawns, and I know she's done for the night.

"Let's get you to bed."

"My bed."

"Sounds good to me." I grin.

"Alone."

My smile vanishes.

"You can't hide from me forever."

Twenty-Four

Alexa

The silence hangs heavily between us as we make our way to my place. My mind and heart are in chaos as conflicting emotions consume me, leaving me torn and worn out.

The desire to trust him and reclaim what we had when we were teens consumes me, even though I know our current dynamic will never be the same as we had before. Perhaps I don't want it to be. Both of us have transformed and grown since our youth and fit better now than we ever would have if none of the other bullshit had happened.

But the only thing I know for certain is if I go home with him now, I'll let him do just about anything he wants with me. There wouldn't be any objections on my part, and that's not the way I want this to work.

My thighs rub together, remembering his earlier closeness. His creative way of still getting what he wanted but not pushing me too far. If anything, he pushed exactly where he needed to—driving me absolutely crazy and over the edge to where I would have let him do many more things to me. And for that reason, we need to take a step back. It may seem illogical, given our recent actions and upcoming nuptials, but I can't dispel this sense of unreadiness.

The car stops, and I go for the handle.

"No," he murmurs.

Confused, I glance over at him, only to see him closing his car door and heading toward my side.

The car door opens, and he looks down at me while offering his hand. I'm thrown into the past.

7 YEARS AGO

I grab Gage's hand like a lifeline as he pulls me from his car outside my house.

"Thank you," I say as I wipe the moisture from my eyes.

Despite Marco's absence, I placed second out of twenty-eight competitors in the finals of my swim meet. Mom and Dad had to go out of town for a funeral and Rosie had a dance competition. Marco promised he'd be there for me since no one else could, but he let me down once again. He's been doing that a lot lately. Dad would've never done that to Mom.

Gage's gaze meets mine as I stand before him, his bottom lip anxiously caught between his teeth. "You did amazing tonight, Lex. You should be proud of yourself. I know I'm proud of you."

I feel another tear escape my eye and trickle down my cheek. Gage's thumb comes to my rescue, wiping it away. I lean into his gentle touch. The comfort it gives is instant.

My second-place metal is now sandwiched between our two bodies, and for some reason, I wish it wasn't there.

I don't want the barrier between us.

Our eyes connect, and I experience a deep desire for Gage to be the one I'm destined to be with forever.

I can always count on him to come through for me, without fail. He didn't have to support me tonight, but he did. He always does. I had a moment of sadness earlier when I looked into the crowd while receiving my metal. No one was there, but as my eyes scanned, I saw him off to the side with a smirk on his face and a package in his hand. At that moment, I felt a familiar wave of calm wash over me, the kind of ease that only he can bring.

In the future, he'll be the reason behind another girl's smile. The thought fills me with a mix of sadness and envy.

What if he marries Rocco's little sister, Gia? She's a couple of years younger than us and is just as crazy as her brother. Gage might like her. I don't want him to like her, though, or any other girl, for that matter.

"Hey, everything's going to be okay," he says as another tear falls from my eye, but this tear isn't for me. This tear is for Gage's fake marriage I just created in my head. "No guy is worth your tears. Brother or not, he doesn't deserve them," he murmurs, thinking I'm crying about his brother when, really, I'm crying at the thought of losing him to another girl one day.

He wraps an arm around me and directs me to my front door.

"Let's get you inside. I saw you eyeing that entremont on the way home," he says with a smile as he holds up the dessert he bought me.

My favorite dessert. One day he'll surprise someone else with her favorite dessert. Sometimes life is so unfair.

I scrunch my nose until I sense him gazing down at me and try to offer him a small smile.

"You still want to go shopping for your dress for the dance tomorrow, yeah?" he asks, probably trying to get my mind off tonight.

"Yeah." I sigh.

Gage insists on accompanying me all the way to my door. Exhausted, I surrender without resistance, allowing him to lead me along.

As I pull my key from my bag, I notice Gage is already inside my place. I thought I locked it earlier.

I step past the threshold and into utter chaos. The once pristine brown leather couch now bears the marks of multiple knife stabbings. The few frames I brought with me are nothing more than broken shards of glass on the ground.

My heart hammers against my ribs as I reach my bedroom door and freeze. There isn't one thing in place. Broken wood pieces surround the dresser drawers, which were once filled with clothes. Feathers cover every surface from remnants of shredded pillows and my down comforter. But what has my stomach in my throat is the dozens of roses thrown on my bed with all of my panties, which seem shredded too.

I join Gage at the foot of my bed, where he's examining everything, and then I pick up a pair of my panties to inspect them.

Regret washes over me in an instant when I feel the sensation of something wet and gooey. I shriek and throw them down before rubbing my hand against my dress repeatedly. I almost give myself a rug burn but don't care in the slightest as long as I get that off my hand.

What the fuck.

"I'll give you five minutes to collect your clothes and anything else you want to bring. You're coming home with me." His jaw tightens, and the gun in his right hand trembles as he instructs me.

The idea of objecting enters my thoughts, but the intensity in his eyes makes me think twice. I can sense the simmering rage just beneath the surface, and I have no desire to provoke it right now.

"Okay. But I'll leave the clothes. I want nothing on my body that this person has touched."

Gage nods his head. "We'll go shopping tomorrow. Five minutes."

"You can take the first room on the right. It was Ro's when she stayed here. I have to make a few calls." He turns, walks into his office, and shuts the door.

I ascend the stairs to the room which will be mine and settle on the bed's edge. With my body trembling and my stomach still experiencing the sickening sensation from my place being ransacked, I cross my arms over my stomach and lean over, taking deep breaths until it passes.

Why would someone do this to me? I haven't had time to make any enemies.

The disgusting display on my bed made it personal. The person responsible has to be the same person who's been following me and leaving roses at my door. And their behavior is becoming more extreme and brazen. I'm terrified of what their next move will be.

There's a light tap on the door, and I raise my eyes to see Gage. "I'm sure you want to shower and sleep. I can give you some of my clothes until tomorrow."

"Okay."

I rise and trail behind him down the hall and into his walk-in closet. He retrieves an oversized black shirt and a pair of his black boxer briefs from a drawer and hands them to me.

"You can take a shower in here. I don't think I have anything in the other bathroom for you to use."

"Okay," I whisper, my gaze falling upon the clothes in my trembling hands.

His index and middle finger gently lift my face to meet his gaze. "Hey, everything will be okay."

Tears fill my eyes as I gaze up at him, making it hard to see, but I nod.

With a gentle tug on my arm, he pulls me into his warm embrace. His powerful arms wrap around me, holding me close as my head finds its place against his chest. I breathe in deeply and anchor myself to the safety he provides.

"Thank you," I whisper.

"I got you," he says as he kisses the top of my head. "I always got you."

As I wake up later, the darkness of the room envelops me. I reach for my phone on the nightstand and see it's a little past two in the morning. After a long struggle to initially fall asleep, I'm now fully awake, extremely tired, and can't close my eyes.

Somewhere in the house, a gentle tune plays, its notes barely audible but enough to capture my attention. I peel the covers away from my warm body and shiver as the cool air hits my skin, peering down the dimly lit hall.

A soft, warm light spills out from Gage's room. With light footsteps, I make my way to his room and cautiously peer inside. He sits with his back against his headboard and his laptop on his lap. From the furrowed brow and thunderous typing, he seems like he's busy, so I turn around.

"Hey, are you okay?"

I turn back toward him. "I can't sleep."

"You can come in here if you'd like." He pats the other side of the bed. "I have a little work to do, but you can watch TV."

"That's okay. Maybe I can sit and listen to music while you work, though?"

"Of course," he says as he places his laptop on his duvet and moves to the other side of the bed while I stand there, watching his every move.

As his sweatpants dangle loosely from his hips, I can't help but admire the alluring contours of his body, now illuminated by the gentle glow. He's dangerously perfect. His body is like a loaded gun. Smooth but hard. Lethal and deadly, depending on the one who's holding it, and Gage knows that. Making him the most dangerous person of all. The thought of him being my husband makes heat appear on my cheeks.

He walks to his mini fridge and pulls out a water bottle before walking it over to me.

"Thanks," I say as I grab it and examine his outstretched inner forearm, where I see a tattoo that sticks out among the rest.

My eyes widen as I gaze up at him.

"Is that...?"

"Yeah, you like it? It was my first tattoo."

I rub my finger along my name in a beautiful cursive font. "I don't know what to say."

"You being speechless is more than enough." He chuckles as he walks to his side of the bed.

His side? What the hell am I saying? I walk to the other side of the bed and try not to consider it mine. His bed is like a cloud, and I sink into its plushness immediately.

I peer at him. "I can't believe you got my name tattooed on you. Are you freaking crazy?"

"Only for you," he smirks as he types.

"Well, don't expect me to get yours."

"Wouldn't dream of it." He smirks.

"What are you doing?"

"Nothing important." He shuts his laptop. "Let's watch a movie. Scary or funny?"

"Funny." I can't handle scary after the horror of my place earlier.

"Snacks?" He quirks his eyebrow.

"Duh."

The lights dim to blackness from an app on his phone as the movie begins to play. The opening credits are all I need to see to know it's one of his favorites and a movie we've watched a million times.

"You would!"

"It's a classic," he says while he lights up a joint and rests it between his lips.

I eye him as he pulls it from his mouth. "You want some?"

I shake my head. "I tried it once with Jenna and it wasn't that great."

"You obviously had some outdoor dirt," he says with a smirk and a twinkle in his eyes. "Let me try something."

"What?"

"Trust me," he says as he brings the joint back to his lips and inhales. Without warning, he leans closer to me and our lips collide. I open the slightest bit, and he blows the smoke beyond my lips. I close my eyes and inhale deeply as his lips leave mine before blowing the smoke out of my lungs. The sensation of floating overcomes me almost instantly as I open my eyes and smile at him.

Holy shit, he just did that shotgun thing I've seen in movies, and it was just as sexy as it seemed on screen.

"We had trash," I say with a smile before giggling. Why am I giggling? This makes him laugh deeply while holding his tight, tattooed abs.

Moments like this fill me with nostalgia. Thousands of memories collide and leave me with a sense of happiness I haven't experienced in longer than I can remember.

The bed dips as Gage gets up. I keep my eyes forward and act like I'm watching the movie even though I haven't paid attention to a single scene since it started.

"Here." He holds out a bar of chocolate. I gaze down at it before snatching it out of his hand.

"Trying to get brownie points or what?"

"I can think of more pleasurable ways to earn brownie points, Lex," he murmurs as he gets back into bed and much closer to me than before.

My stomach does a flip at the use of my nickname. This is the first time I've heard him say it since we were younger, and it does things to me, things I'm not willing to admit to myself.

I ignore him and break off a piece of chocolate, then place it on my tongue and moan as the velvety goodness melts instantly.

I catch him gazing at me with a weird expression on his face. "What?"

"Nothing."

I hold the chocolate bar up. "I'll give you a piece if you can be a good boy."

He licks his lips as he looks over at me. "Where's the fun in that?"

"Guess you aren't getting any, then." I shrug. His hand shoots out as he attempts to grab my chocolate, but I hold it to my side as I lean away. "Nope, none for you."

Gage jumps on top of me with a quickness I don't expect. His thighs lock my legs closed while his hands grip my wrists, holding me in place. My chocolate bar stands vertical in my hands above my head.

"You were saying?" He arches a brow.

"Bad boys don't deserve chocolate."

Gage leisurely scans my body under him. "But bad girls do?"

"I'm not a bad girl."

"No, you're my good girl, aren't you?" he says in a velvety voice that sounds better than my chocolate tastes.

My cheeks heat and I turn my head away from his intense stare. He leans above me and takes a huge bite out of my chocolate bar.

"Hey!" I shriek as the piece of chocolate hangs from his mouth.

He dips his head and places the other side against my lips. I open my mouth and bite the piece off, my eyes never leaving his.

This is unlike any other moment we've experienced. It's not charged by hatred, tension, or lust.

This is two friends finally taking the plunge into the next phase of their relationship.

This is what I imagine our first moments would have been like if all the other shit wouldn't have happened.

I lift my head, offering myself to him, and he complies as his mouth comes down on mine. It's reminiscent of our first kiss in the garden, tender and unhurried. Like we're still unsure, but savoring the moment. His mouth is an intoxicating mix of chocolate and smoke, and I never want it to stop.

Twenty-Five

Gage

With a smirk on my face, I observe Alexa's frustrated huff as she regains her stance, determination clear in her eyes. Under the hexagon lights in my home gym, her body glistens, clad only in her bra and my boxer briefs. After our movie last night, she made excuses and retreated to the other room, much to my disappointment, so I woke her up early for a sparring session.

"Why are we doing this? Aren't you supposed to protect me as my soon-to-be husband?"

"I will, but I want to know that you're capable of fighting if something happens to me."

She crinkles her nose. "Don't say things like that."

"It's always a possibility. You know how this life is. A new day is never guaranteed."

"Well, I don't like to think about it."

"Careful, Lex. Your love for me is going to make my heart burst," I say with a smirk.

She glares at me as she prepares to attack. I dodge her jab, then wrestle her down to the ground.

"I knew this was your plan all along," she says as she gazes up at me.

"It was part of it." I laugh.

"And the other part?" she asks with a quirk of her eyebrow.

"When I found out about what happened to you, I felt so guilty I wasn't there to protect you. We could've lost you," I say as I rub my finger against the raised scar near her ear. I know she's ashamed of the scar and what it represents, but she shouldn't be. It shows her strength and resilience.

She flips me onto my side. "It wasn't your fault. You didn't have a choice—"

"I always had a choice. I was just too weak to go against it."

"You were never—"

"I was." I feel the scar running long and raised across my palm.

The reminder of the day I finally showed myself is seared into my flesh.

16 YEARS OLD

My father cuts my palm and I wince at the initial sting as he looks into my eyes. "Pathetic," he spits with disgust.

His new objective has been to inflict pain until Marco and I no longer wince or flinch or move. He intends for us to turn into nonfeeling robots just like him.

It's an exhausting mind game, and I'm sick of it.

The blackness seeps into my soul as it always does, but this time, I don't push it back down.

My fingers clench around the knife, still deeply embedded in my flesh, and I pull it closer. Ignoring the searing pain that rips through me, which passes as the black haze fades it into nothingness.

"Let the blade go, Gage," my father says through clenched teeth as he tries to pry it from my hand.

I squeeze the blade in my palm harder until my crimson blood creates more of a stream and less of a trickle on his desk.

"You wanted blood. Let there be blood," I say in a voice that seems foreign.

Marco comes into my line of sight behind our father and shakes his head for me to stop while holding his bleeding palm.

I'm sick of seeing him get hurt. I'm sick of getting hurt. This has to stop.

A smile reaches my lips as I flick my eyes back to my father while taking in his reaction. The fear in his eyes is something I've never witnessed in him.

I let his words and his beliefs of my unworthiness turn me into the monster he tried to craft me to be. What he didn't know is that this side of me was there all along, fighting to come out, fighting to dance with the light I shrouded myself in.

He learned the mistake he made today, and fuck, it feels good.

She grabs my hand, bringing me back to the present.

"Jesus, Gage, what is that?" Alexa says as she runs her finger along the scar.

"A reminder of who I am. Come on, we'll go get you some new clothes, and then we have to get ready for the meeting."

Manuel, Tony, and Rocco file into the room later that day, but what confuses me is Gia trailing the three of them.

"This was to be a closed conversation," I say as I glare at Gia. She will never be in a position of power, so I don't understand her attendance today when we're speaking of important matters.

"We've already got one woman in here. What's the difference?" Manuel mutters.

I don't need to glance at Alexa to know the comment stung.

"Alexa may be a capo as you three are, but the difference is she is to be my wife. This puts her higher in rank and importance, and she deserves the same respect as you. I won't put up with anything less."

The transition of putting a woman in a boss's role hasn't been smooth, though I'd never mention that to her. These stupid fucks and their fathers need to get out of the Dark Ages. This will happen whether they like it or not.

"Understood, boss," Rocco says with a begrudging huff as he looks at his sister. "Should we begin?"

"Not until Marco arrives." On cue, my brother walks in. The fucker was probably listening on the other side of the door.

"Someone mentioned me?" he asks as he walks in with a smile before coming to stand between Alexa and me.

I narrow my eyes at him, silently warning him to step away from Alexa, but he remains unfazed and unmoving.

I have to get out of this townhouse and into a bigger house with a bigger office. Being crammed in here is making my already bad mood worse.

"Okay, let's get to business. What do you have for me, Rocco?"

He looks over at his sister and then back at me. "There were once whispers of you marrying my sister. Now that is no longer," he says as he looks over at Alexa. "We'd like to propose a marriage between her and Marco now that she's of age."

I observe Marco, who has become as still as a statue, and unfortunately, Alexa, too. Alexa looks over at Marco and then at me before leveling Rocco with a glare. "No."

I feel the air leave my lungs as those two letters, that one simple word, gut punch me.

Did last night mean nothing to her? Will I always be second best to him?

Twenty-Six

Alexa

ROSIE'S WEDDING

"**M**ay I cut in?" Marco asks from the other side of Gage.

I go still in Gage's arms. Throughout the night, I attempted to keep my distance from Marco. While I've moved on from being upset, I still have little interest in being in his presence.

"Absolutely the fuck not," Gage spits.

"It's fine," I say, stepping back. I don't want him to ruin Rosie's day by making a scene. I don't believe he will, but I also don't know. His fuse seems to be a lot shorter than it's ever been.

Gage mutters something to Marco as they have a stare down. I can't help but compare the two as I'm stuck between them. Gage is reminiscent of a fallen angel who screams temptation, sin, and rebellion. While Marco still looks like the boy next door—ordinary, likable, probably writes in a calendar and irons all of his clothes before he puts them on.

At one point, I believed Marco was the one who made my heart race, but he never did. It was always Gage.

"Graphic, I dig it. No worries, baby bro," Marco says to Gage.

A huge smile graces Marco's lips as he pulls me into his arms. "Laugh as if I said something funny to piss him off."

My head tilts back, and I laugh. Because why the hell not? I'm down to be petty and piss Gage off a little.

"I wanted to apologize," Marco murmurs.

"There's no need."

"There is," he says as he leans closer to my ear. "You will always be one of the most beautiful girls in the room, and I'm sorry for making you feel less than you are. I just never had the courage to tell you I'm-I'm only attracted to men."

I pull back and look into his eyes that are a mix of sorrow and vulnerability.

"But I saw you."

"You walked in on me with someone who had long brown hair," he says as he looks over to the right.

I follow his gaze and land on my older cousin, Vinny. His long brown hair in a tight ponytail at the back of his head. With a scowl on his face, he skillfully spins a knife between his fingers, never taking his eyes off us.

"You mean?"

"Yeah," he says as he looks back at my cousin with love in his eyes and a grin on his face. While Vinny still looks two seconds from wanting to stab someone. Probably me. Marco leans back in and whispers in my ear. "Watch."

Vinny gets up from the table, almost knocking over the chair, then storms away.

"He's such a drama queen sometimes."

I smile up at Marco. "I should've known. Good luck with my cousin. From the looks of it, you're going to need it."

"I can handle him," he says with a smile. "Are we all good?"

"Yes. I hope you two will be happy."

All of his erratic behavior when we were younger makes sense. He went about it the wrong way, but he was hurting.

"You know we can't be together. Only in secret."

"It doesn't need to be like that. We'll talk to Gage. You both deserve happiness and acceptance. Love is between hearts—"

Marco pulls me into the tightest hug I think I've ever received.

"Thank you..." he whispers as he takes a deep breath. "Your dad's coming, and I'd rather not have another chat with him. I hope you and Gage will be happy, too."

"Yeah, I don't know about that," I say as I glance over at Gage regarding us with an expression I can't decipher, but it makes my stomach flutter. Why does he do this to me?

"Gage may be different, but his heart is still the same. It's only ever beat for you. Give him hell, but give him a chance. After everything, he deserves it."

"You can't swap brothers on a whim, Alexa. This isn't your decision," Manuel sneers.

"Fuck you!"

"I don't like sloppy thirds," Manuel spits back at me.

Gage's gun is out of its holster and aimed at Manuel before I can blink.

Tony's eyes widen in shock as he raises his hands and positions himself as a shield between his brother and the gun, which is ominously aimed at his sibling's head. "He didn't mean it. Rocco, let's table this discussion. We have time. Gia, why don't you go out to the living room? We'll be out soon."

She looks over at Marco and then her gaze shifts to me while her mouth turns into a sneer. I give her the same, my eyes piercing with a mix of annoyance and amusement, and then a smirk forms on my lips as she walks out of the room.

I've never liked Gia. She's self-centered, spoiled, and a total bitch. I went to her birthday party at her house last year and that was all I needed to see. She yelled at the house staff because "they were beneath her" as she said. And when she didn't get the car she wanted, she threw a fit and actually stomped her feet. No way am I letting Marco end up with her, even if I didn't know he was in love with my older cousin.

Gage places his gun on the desk with a heavy clunk while its barrel stays aimed toward them. The unspoken warning hangs in the air.

As Tony moves back to his seat, Manuel averts his eyes, making a conscious effort to avoid looking toward me and Gage. Good.

"Alexander Petrov's shipments should reach both docks Wednesday at nine forty-five. See that everything goes smoothly. Bring extra detail just in case," Gage says. "I want a detailed inventory of everything that makes it to land."

"We're really working with the Russians?" Tony's eyebrow shoots up.

I, too, am shocked. I only met the Petrovs briefly when I was younger while in Italy. The only thing I remember was tension. Steeped in old-world values, the Russians are part of a secret society whose deplorable deeds rival our own.

"It expands our reach. We have access to the ports in Los Angeles again, and our revenue in the gun and drug trade will double. Unless you don't want the extra money?" Gage says.

"What about the Stockade? Will that open back up now that we're working with the Russians?" Manuel asks with a smile on his face, which makes me sick. I never went, but I know what it is, and I'm glad it burned to the ground.

"Absolutely not. Anyone who traffics while I'm in charge will be executed."

You could hear a pin drop with how silent the room falls. No one says anything, so Gage continues, "Hector placed a hit. He wouldn't divulge who it was for, but the amount was steep, so it could be for multiple people."

The thought of Gage's father leaves an acrid taste in my mouth, and I can't help but imagine bringing him back to life solely to repeat the act of killing him myself. I'm just thankful my dad's okay, and his plan never got carried out.

"What do you have for me?" Gage looks over at Marco, who's now his underboss. He wanted out, but there's no way out for us. He's always been the best at mingling, charming, and learning secrets, so that's what he now does.

"I've heard more noise from my contact. The hit man, as-sassin, or whatever you want to call him is in town and has been for a while. Allegedly, he's one of the best and has never fucked up a kill. There's some vendetta or some shit, so it's personal, which means we're fucked."

"We find out who it is and pay them off." Rocco shrugs as if it's that easy.

"If it's personal, a vendetta, as Marco says, we're fucked. Would you allow someone to pay you off and forgo exacting your revenge?" Gage asks with a raised brow.

The room falls silent. All of them too bloodthirsty at the thought of revenge to be paid off. Some infractions are priceless. No amount of money can satisfy that.

Everyone besides Gage, Marco, and me leave because we have close to nothing to go on aside from what we already know and the new fact that someone shot at Manuel last week. He's a monster, so I'm sure he has more people gunning for him than just an assassin.

"Well, I have places to be, so I'll just be going," Marco says as he stands.

The telltale sound of a gun's safety echoes in the room as the tip of Gage's gun presses against the side of Marco's head.

"Gage! What are you doing?" I say as I rise to my feet, my heart pounding outside of my chest.

"What's going on between you two?"

"Nothing. Put the gun down!" I say as I move to look at Gage's face. His eyes seem lifeless, devoid of the customary mischievous sparkle I've grown fond of.

"You almost had me fooled," Gage says as he looks at me. "You—"

"What the hell is going on?" Marco says with his hands up in surrender.

"Do you want him?" Gage asks me.

I frown. "No."

"Then why? Why say no earlier?"

Say no to what? As I try to make sense of what he's saying, I scan the room, then shift my gaze toward Marco again. Shit.

"Because—he isn't going to marry her."

"Why?" Gage barks.

"He—"

"I'm not attracted to her or Alexa," Marco murmurs.

"You stupid mother—"

"I'm in love with Vinny," Marco says as a tear drops to his cheek.

Gage's eyes shift from me to Marco.

"You're gay?" Gage asks, perplexed, as he removes his gun from Marco's face and takes a step back.

"Yes," Marco whispers as his eyes hit the floor.

"Why didn't you tell me?" Gage asks with hurt in his voice.

"I was scared. You know how it is in this family."

"I'd never do anything. You have to know that. Is this why Vinny was so willing to betray our father and work both sides?"

"Yes. He was trying to protect me."

"Did our father know?"

Marco looks sullen as he nods. "Why do you think he spent so much time with me? He was trying to change my mind."

"Fuck," Gage says as he rubs a hand down his face. "I'm sorry. I didn't know."

"It's all good," Marco says as he walks to the door while wiping his cheek.

"Marco," Gage barks. "I don't care who the fuck you love as long as it's not my girl. You will always be welcome, no matter what. I'll kill anyone who says otherwise."

A tear threatens to leak from my eye as I watch a shift happen in their relationship for the better. I knew Gage would understand.

Twenty-Seven

Alexa

"You didn't have to come with me," I say as I glance over at Gage in the driver's seat. Rosie and Vic cut their honeymoon short and came home since Rosie wasn't feeling well, so I wanted to go see her and make sure she's okay. Gage decided he was coming before I even extended the invite. Not that I really mind.

"Already trying to get rid of me?" Gage asks with a grin.

"I didn't say that," I say as I give him a good up and down. He's in dark denim jeans and a black Henley, which shows off the extensive gray and black ink on his upper chest and neck. I like this look on him. He looks relaxed and almost approachable compared to his usual imposing demeanor in three-piece suits.

"Vic, Trey, and I have business, and I'd like to see my sister. Make sure he's still treating her well."

"You know he is," I say as I smile and shake my head. His endearing big brother protectiveness makes me long for a sibling of my own. I wonder how different my life would have been if I had someone to protect me like he's done for Rosie.

"Yeah, well, I'm still pissed at him for keeping everything from me."

"Doesn't feel good, does it?" I joke, but his face immediately changes to a frown as he turns to me and places his hand on my thigh. I instantly regret my words.

"I'll forever be sorry for lying to you."

"I know," I say, gazing out the window. I want to get past this. Past the hurt, past the uncertainty. All of us need to heal from one thing or another, but we can't if it keeps getting brought up. I know I need to make a conscious decision to move past this, just as Gage needs to get past the way Marco hurt him.

I place my hand over his as I redirect my gaze back to him. "You know, what you did earlier probably made Marco's whole year. You can tell your acceptance meant a lot to him."

"I wish it would have come out a little differently. I feel like an asshole for pulling a gun on him and putting him in that position. Now, knowing what I know, that's not the brother or person I'd like to be."

"Is it at all surprising to you?"

"A little..." Gage says as he seems thoughtful for a second with a scrunch of his brow. "I never understood why Vinny sought me out the moment I got out. He was always so loyal to my father, but when I saw him, he practically begged me to let him come on and take him down. In the beginning, it was suspicious, but I gave him a chance, and he never faltered. Never did anything to make me question his motives."

I nod, understanding. "His love for Marco made him seek you out. I'm positive he knew you'd be open-minded about Marco's choice of love, just like I was sure you'd accept him."

"Like I said, I don't care who he loves. He's my twin, and at one point, we were close. We all were," Gage mutters, then shakes his head. "As long as he's happy and treated well, that's all that matters. Everyone deserves happiness. Even the worst of us."

"Agreed," I say with a smile.

"After we leave my sister's, I want to take you to the club."

My eyes widen at his quick change of thought. The club and his intentions for me at said club make my nerves run wild. "I don't know—"

"Do you trust me?" he asks as he glances at me. I gaze out the window as I contemplate life recently. I do trust he won't hurt me, but I don't know if I trust his full honesty yet. Last night felt so right. It was the closest I've seen him act like the boy I once knew. And I promised myself I'd let the hurt go, but still.

"Yes and no," I say honestly, because every time I think about it, I still find a "but" in my thought process.

"What can I do to make you trust me?"

"Time."

His upper lip picks up a fraction as he looks over at me and grabs my thigh roughly, causing butterflies to invade my belly. "Time is something we have a lot of. I can deal with that."

When we arrive at Vic and Rosie's house, I rush to the room Vic gestures to, paying no attention to the guys.

"Okay, spill, there's no way you're too sick to be in the Maldives with a bikini on, toes in the sand, and a piña colada in hand," I say as soon as I walk into the room. She smiles as she looks at me, and

I study her messy bun and pale face as she sits in bed, clutching a bowl in her lap.

Her hand goes into her front hoodie pocket. "Close your eyes and open your hand."

I place my left hand over my eyes and outstretch my right hand. A featherlight plastic object lands on my palm, causing me to uncover my eyes and glance downward, where I find a positive pregnancy test.

"Surprise, Auntie Alexa."

"No fucking way!" I say as I jump on the bed next to Rosie and pull her in for a hug. She's going to be a mom. Gage is going to be an uncle, and I'm going to be an aunt. I'm so excited.

"I said the same thing as I threw up in the toilet earlier."

"How does Vic feel about it?"

"He's ecstatic. I think he was trying to get me pregnant from day one," she says with a silly smile. I love that my best friend is in love.

"It happened so quick."

"We didn't use protection. Don't remind him, though, his head is already big enough as it is," she mutters as she rolls her eyes, making us both laugh.

We sit around discussing what the gender could be and possible baby names until the door slams against the wall, making us both jump. Jenna comes into the room with a limp. She's disheveled from head to toe, no shoes on her feet, with dirt and blood caked everywhere.

"Jenna, are you okay?" I ask as I walk over to her.

"I'm sorry. I really tried," she says with a grimace as she pulls her palm away from her right thigh, which is covered in blood. She grabs the edge of her long-sleeved black shirt and rips the whole sleeve off, then wraps it around her wound before pulling it tight with a grimace.

"What are you talking about? What happened?"

"There isn't enough time," she says, shaking her head.

"You aren't making any sense. You need to see a doctor for your leg. It's bleeding bad." I point at her blood-soaked thigh, which needs stitches, and quick from the way the makeshift tourniquet is already soaked in blood.

"Shit, get on the bed. Now!" she hisses as she pushes me away. I slip in my socks and fall back onto the hardwood floor with a thud while I regard her as if she's lost her fucking mind.

In a split second, Jenna takes her place quietly by the wall. As Rosie gasps, my gaze follows hers, and I spot a figure entering the room. Their black tactical boots announce their presence with a menacing squeak. My eyes gradually travel upward, taking in the sight of someone dressed in black cargo pants, a black shirt, and a mask that obscures their face. As I scramble to grab my knife, my fingers close around... nothing... Panic sets in when I remember not bringing it along, relying on Gage to keep me safe. When am I going to learn my damn lesson?

The guy takes two steps in our direction, causing Rosie to release a bloodcurdling scream. That gives Jenna enough time to creep up behind him, jump on his back, pull up his mask, and slice him across his throat from ear to ear. I watch the blood trickle down his neck as he drops to his knees, prompting Jenna to gracefully jump off him before he falls face-first onto the floor.

"Jesus fucking Christ, Jenna!"

"I'm sorry," she mutters, out of breath as she takes her knife and cleans it against her black pants before placing it into her back pocket. What in the hell is going on?

I clamber to the side of the bed and use it to help myself up, then I glance over at Rosie, whose ragged breath was almost to the point of hyperventilating. I crawl on the bed and grab her arm, which is quaking with the rest of her body. "Ro, it's okay. You're safe."

She looks right through me as if I'm not in front of her, which scares the hell out of me. The memories of her recent attack and abduction must be flooding back, causing her to relive the trauma all over again. I know little about being pregnant, but I'm sure this isn't good for her or the baby.

"Rosie. Look at me," I murmur as I grab her hands in mine. They're clammy and cold, but once I have a good grip on them, she looks at me and not through me. "That's good," I say in a soothing tone. "We're going to breathe together. Let's breathe in for three seconds and then out for three. Okay?"

She blinks, but not much else. We do three sets of the breathing exercises together, which usually helps me. She calms down slightly, but I'm still worried. "You're doing great. Let's keep taking those breaths, okay?"

I'm still aware of Jenna's presence and the dead guy in the room, but my focus is solely on making sure Rosie gets through this. It's odd how this doesn't faze me, yet the mere thought of someone trailing me in my car turns me into a complete wreck. Each of us carries our own traumas, but they manifest in unique ways. I just hope I'm able to get Rosie through hers so I can focus on what's happening behind me.

"I think I'm going to be sick," Rosie says right before she throws up into the bowl between us while I'm still holding her hands.

The distinct sound of shuffling catches my attention, and I glance around. Jenna flips the guy onto his back, then rips his mask off his face.

"Ah, Paul. I have to hand it to you. You got me good this time," she says as she pats his bloody cheek.

"What the fuck is going on, Jenna?" I ask as I watch her fish her phone out of her bra and take a picture of the dead guy.

Rosie gasps.

Jenna says nothing as she roots around in the guy's pockets. I grab Rosie a tissue from her nightstand, then walk over to Jenna and grab her arm. "What is going on, and how the hell did you jump on that guy's back and slit his throat like it was nothing?"

She looks at me with regret in her eyes. "I have to go."

"What do you mean?"

"It means more are coming, and I have to kill them all."

"Wait," Rosie says as she gets up from the bed. "You saved Jess and me that night."

Jenna looks over at Rosie. "I did."

I hear footsteps echo from down the hall as Gage and Vic come in with their guns raised. Vic runs over to Rosie and wraps her in his arms as Gage points his gun directly between Jenna's eyes. "You aren't going fucking anywhere until you tell us what's going on."

Jenna doesn't bat an eye as Gage's Glock sits a few feet from her face. Silence falls across the room before she huffs out a deep breath, "I was tasked to eliminate the Mafia families of Chicago."

I rip my hand off her arm and stumble back as if I've been burned while Gage's jaw ticks and tightens. He moves more into the room, but never takes his finger off the trigger.

"You? You were going to kill me?" I ask as my throat closes, and I feel like I've been kicked in the stomach.

Jenna's eyes soften the slightest bit as she looks at me. "It was supposed to be easy, but then I got something I've never had before... family."

My lips tremble, and I step toward her, but Gage takes a step forward, so he's between her and I.

"When were you planning on slitting Alexa's throat? Or mine? Or my sister's?" Gage asks in a deadly calm tone as the cool metal of his gun rests against her forehead. Again, Jenna doesn't flinch or appear even remotely worried.

"If I wanted you dead, you'd be dead." Jenna's hands move so fast, it barely registers. One minute, the gun is against her forehead, and the next, her index finger holds it up in front of Gage's face at the trigger guard. "Like I said, more are coming, and I plan to kill them all." She hands Gage his gun back and then grabs the mountain of a man by the arm and begins to pull him out into the hall.

"How many?" Gage asks.

"A lot. I didn't execute the job. Now they're coming for me and all of you," Jenna says as she huffs out a sigh, then looks at both Gage and Vic. "This house isn't safe. You all need to move somewhere else until this is handled."

"Wait!" I say as I walk around Gage to follow her.

Jenna looks back at me with pain in her eyes. "I don't have many happy memories, but what I do have while being here, with you girls, are amazing. You are strong, Alexa. Never forget that."

Tears line my eyes, and my heart catches in my throat as Jenna turns back to the dead guy with a limp and pulls him out of the room and toward the hallway.

"We have to help her," Rosie says as she argues with Gage.

"No. I don't trust her," Gage says.

"Neither do I," Vic mutters.

"She saved Jess and me that night, Vic. She was the girl in the mask. If it wasn't for her, we'd be dead."

"She also saved us now," I say a little louder so they can hear me as I walk over the threshold.

"If I can have just one day, one fucking day—" Gage mutters.

Avoiding the red trail that runs down the hall, I cringe as I carefully step over it. This is a disgusting mess, and the metallic scent makes me want to use Rosie's bucket to hurl.

"We meet again, Red. Is this a present for me?" Trey says to Jenna with a smirk on his face as he takes the last step onto the second-floor landing.

She looks over at him in disgust. "I don't have time for your games today, baldy."

His smile widens. "You love our games."

Jenna huffs and then winces as she limps to him. "Then our game today is you getting rid of the body. I cook, you clean."

She tries to walk past him, but he grabs her wrist, causing her to stop in her tracks. "Are you okay?"

Jenna whispers something before shaking him off and walking down the stairs. Trey shakes his head as he unzips the duffel in his hand and unfolds a tarp. He smiles as he tilts the guy's chin to look at Jenna's handiwork, and I decide that's my cue. Apparently, everyone around me is a psychopath.

I walk back into the room, leaving Trey in the hall with the dead guy just as Gage gets off the phone. "Is your lake house complete?"

"Almost. Done enough to stay there," Vic says as he holds Rosie close.

"Good." Gage nods as he looks around and then back at his sister and Vic. "You never told me why you cut your three-week vacation I paid for short. You two would be a lot safer two oceans away," Gage says.

My gaze falls to Rosie, who's watching Vic, who wears the biggest smile I've ever seen. "You're going to be an uncle."

Gage's facial expression changes before my eyes, shifting from confusion to contemplation to shock and finally settling into anger.

Gage takes a predatory step toward Vic. "I'm not too well-versed in how long these things take, but I believe a week or so from your wedding would be a little too soon to tell, don't you think?"

"You wouldn't want to hit your niece or nephew's dad. Would you?" Vic says with a grin as I watch Rosie's face drain of color.

"I'm going to kill—"

My fingers clench around Gage's arm. "I thought you were taking me to the club."

Gage gazes down at me, and his eyes lose their edge as his body softens. Then, he looks back over at Vic and Rosie. "Congratulations, baby sister. Vic, keep my sister and the baby safe. Also, go fuck yourself."

Rosie manages a mouthed, "Thank you," as I quickly pull Gage out of the room, avoiding any further awkwardness.

Did I just offer my body on a silver platter to help my best friend? I sure did. Let's hope I don't regret it.

Twenty-Eight

Gage

My body is electrified with a rush of adrenaline as I fix my eyes on Alexa, gracefully suspended in the sex swing. With her red-painted toes nestled in the black stirrups while she clutches the handles with her hands. She lies bare, save for the small black lingerie set that clings to her curves and a black fabric mask covering her eyes.

The drive from Indiana to the club was torturous. Each minute that passed was like a ticking time bomb.

Would Alexa change her mind?

Would she back out?

I kept her busy by talking about Rosie and the baby. I still can't believe I'm going to have a niece or nephew. The stupid motherfucker got her pregnant before they were married, and I'm tempted to kill him for it.

In a Mafia arranged marriage, there are certain expectations, a pure wife being one. That expectation is archaic and dumb in my opinion, but if Rosie and Vic hadn't reconciled, and I had to arrange a marriage to keep her safe, we would have had a serious problem. One being her lack of virginity, and two, a baby already in her womb.

Then there's the Jenna problem. I don't trust her, haven't from the beginning, but Alexa does, and she pleaded her friend's case until we reached the club.

Once we got here, reality sank in, and she tried to backpedal.

"So, what? You want to control me?"

"Yes—"

Her eyes widen before narrowing into slits.

"It's not what you think," I say. "You give me the control, but it's you who has the control over me."

"I don't follow."

If only I had sought advice on how to explain this to her from Apollo, the club's Dom instructor, things would have been much easier. He patiently passed on his knowledge, teaching me everything I now know. I made a conscious decision to stay away from Alexa until I had absorbed all the knowledge he had to offer. Making this special for her is crucial, so I wanted to ensure I did it perfectly. The only thing I never asked about was the best way to broach the subject with her.

"You grant me control, but ultimately, you are the one with the power. You can say stop at any moment, and I'll stop."

"Then how does that give you control?" she says with a quirked brow.

"You give me the control to know what you need and when you need it, but—"

"I'm in control," she finishes.

"Yes."

So here I stand in my black boxer briefs, with soft red satin sheets under my bare feet, pillows scattered around the firm mattress, and a riding crop in my hand.

I take a step forward and touch the leather end of the riding crop against her neck, then trail it between her breasts. The surprising touch of the cold leather causes her to intake a breath of surprise before swallowing.

"Deep breath, baby. You're safe," I murmur.

She huffs, and I can't help but grin at her little attitude. Despite her nerves, I can sense her underlying trust in me, which is the only reason we're doing this now. It's another means for us to strengthen our connection.

I continue my descent down her torso and hop to her inner left thigh. Goose bumps pepper her skin as she releases a moan of satisfaction. I mirror the movements onto her right thigh, but stay away from the place she really wants the crop to touch. The spot I want to touch.

"What's the word, Lex?"

"Red."

"That's a good girl," I say and watch a small smile spread across her face. "If you say it, this stops. You're in charge."

I remove the crop from her skin as I grab the remote from the mattress and turn it on to the lowest setting. The telltale sound of the small vibrator against her clit buzzes to life, making her moan loud as her head bows back.

"Just feel, beautiful."

Gripping the crop in my right hand, I feel a surge of anticipation as I make my first contact with her inner thigh. Her mouth opens on another moan, which matches mine as I see a small pink imprint from the leather. I turn the vibrator to the second setting as I deliver another mark on her other thigh.

I continue alternating between a blow from the crop and a higher setting on the vibrator.

Alexa sits in the swing with her head tilted back and moans bouncing off the walls of the room which rival the music playing. Her fists are clenching the handles in a death grip while she licks her dry lips. Her quivering and shaking spurs me on. I accelerate the dial to the highest level and watch her toes curl as she is seconds from coming apart. I bring the crop down one last time and hit her at the apex of her thighs. Right on the vibrator in her wet thong, which still rests against her clit. She screams as she comes, and it's the most beautiful sound I've ever heard.

I grab my cock for the first time tonight. It's harder and more ready than it's ever been. I thrust it against my palm while I watch Alexa's breath level out.

As I step between her legs, I gently place a hand on her lower back, drawing her closer to me. With a swift motion, I remove her left foot from the stirrup, then her right.

"Remove your hands, Lex," I say as her legs wrap around my waist.

She takes her hands off the straps and wraps them around my neck as I lower us both down to the pillows. I remove her mask and search her eyes.

"Are you sure?"

"Yes," she says with a small smile.

"What do you want?"

"You. Fuck me, Gage."

I search her eyes a second longer for any doubts, but I see none. My lips come down on hers in a hungry kiss. As I pull down my boxer briefs, a sense of urgency courses through me. I decide to move her scrap of black fabric to the side rather than remove it. With her hands still above her head, I grip them and eagerly thrust in.

Similar to the first time, this moment is incredibly intoxicating, overwhelming, and undeniably perfect. But what sets this time apart is her desire for it to be me. Not the guy who sought to impress her with his seductive words and secrets because he feared the rejection. Just me, laying every piece of myself bare for her.

Her eyes shimmer with a vibrant blue, mirroring the start of a brand-new day, a new beginning. Her mouth parts, and she emits a soft, melodic moan that has my knees going weak.

I pull back, then plunge in again while we remain connected in more ways than one. In our eyes, that show more than words will ever say. In our hands, that are intertwined just like our souls are. And in our hearts, that only beat for each other.

"You're such a good girl. So beautiful," I say between grunts and kisses as I thrust into her repeatedly.

Grabbing a satin pillow from the side of the bed, I wedge it under her lower back before plunging back in.

"Oh fuck," she chants as her eyes widen while I pound into her relentlessly at this new angle.

God, she feels so fucking good.

My body falls onto hers as our lips touch again, eager to learn if her moans taste as intoxicating as they sound.

Twenty-Nine

Alexa

With a single fluid motion, Gage flips us over, leaving me straddling him as our bodies remain intertwined. My eyes widen as I feel him even deeper than he was before.

I gaze into his eyes and gave him a questioning expression. The right side of his upper lip pulls into a smirk before his firm hands grab onto my hips, and he rocks me forward onto him. A little bundle of nerves in me gets hit, making my back arch and my eyes roll into the back of my head. It's a dangerously delicious sensation, a high I never want to come down from.

"Eyes on me, beautiful."

With my hands resting on his muscular chest, I can feel his heartbeat against my palms as he skillfully guides me back and forth while my half-lidded eyes remain fixed on him. His face contorts as I use my strength to match his. He reveals a blend of bliss and intense focus as he clenches his lower lip between his teeth and grips my hips tighter.

Witnessing him unraveling beneath me fills me with an over-whelming sense of empowerment. He makes me feel confident, sexy, and strong. I love the way he makes me feel. I love *him*.

The truth settles upon me like a warm blanket as I come to terms with what has always been—my undeniable love for this man.

My body presses against his as we kiss, and I savor the sensation of my clit grazing his lower stomach.

"I love you," I moan as I gaze into his deep-blue eyes.

His eyes widen, and a startled breath escapes his lips before his hands shoot out to grasp my face. "I love you, Lex, so fucking much."

My body rocks harder against his as I'm consumed by a fiery sensation, causing me to moan once again as the pressure builds. "I'm going to come."

As Gage shifts, we align ourselves into a sitting position, our bodies still connected while our hearts throb in unison.

As he bites down on the side of my neck, he whispers, "Be a good girl and come for me." His powerful arms enveloping me in a tight hug as he thrusts deeply, igniting a rush of inexplicable sensations. I come with a scream that has me seeing stars as I feel him thrust twice more before coming inside me with a groan.

We continue to hold each other with our bodies intertwined until our erratic breathing subsides and there's nothing but silence in the room.

"Come on, I want you at home in our bed so I can worship you more."

The word 'our' no longer sounds awful. It sounds like a new beginning and happiness.

243

Ten minutes later, we step out of the club with Gage's arm secured around me. The refreshing chill of the early morning air greets us. I inhale and let a smile creep onto my lips.

"What?" Gage asks as he smirks down at me.

"I never thought it would feel like this."

His dark eyes twinkle with my words as he bends and kisses the side of my head. "I knew it would, and this is only the beginning, Lex."

We make it five steps out when we come to an abrupt halt.

Brad stands ten feet away with a gun aimed in our direction. His hair is in complete disarray, extensive bruising mars his face, and his clothes are in tattered shambles.

"What the fuck are you doing here?" Gage yells.

"It was supposed to be me. You were supposed to end up with me. I watched you for months. Even tried to protect you that night from my brother."

"What are you talking about?" I ask.

"Your father killed my brother the night he chased you. I told him I would keep you. And he wouldn't let me. I always knew I would get you back." He smiles and then fires the gun.

I drop to my knees as Gage grunts out in pain and falls back while holding his stomach.

"My... gun..." Gage rasps.

I pull it from the holster on his side and turn, but Brad is already gone.

"Help!" I scream as I hold pressure against his wound. "Help!"

Gage looks up at me with a grimace before his hand reaches my cheek. "I will always love you, Lex."

And then his hand falls to the side.

Two days later

A whirlwind of emotion chokes me while I lie on the small, uncomfortable hospital bed next to Gage. My eyes close as the sound of him flatlining twice in the back of the ambulance rings through my mind. Unbelievable, gut-wrenching despair echoes in that sound, which will forever haunt me. When he flatlined for the second time, a wave of distress washed over me, and dark, unsettling thoughts crept into my mind. He isn't allowed to leave me when we barely got our second chance. I made a solemn promise to myself that if he didn't survive, I would willingly follow him into the afterlife. Wherever he goes, I go.

I open my eyes and wipe a lone tear as I gaze up at Gage. Even in his medically induced coma, he still looks just as handsome and lethal as always, even though the bullet bounced around in his body, causing substantial damage, and the doctors say it will take months to heal. He has a long road ahead of him, and I will be there the entire way.

From the door, a distinct click reaches my ears, causing my gaze to fixate on Vic and Trey walking into the room.

"Is Rosie safe?" I ask Vic.

"Yeah, we have people with her right now."

"Good," I say as I nod. "I want him found and brought to a secure location. I don't want him roughed up too bad before I see him. He worked with me at Brilliant Hearts Charity, so there should be some kind of information on his whereabouts."

"We'll let you know when we have something."

"Thank you," I say, directing my attention back to Gage.

It's odd giving someone orders, but it seems appropriate, especially if it leads to the apprehension of the person responsible for harming Gage.

As the guys leave, I glance at Marco, slumped over in the rigid, uncomfortable chair. Since they let us into his room after his eight-hour surgery, he has been reluctant to leave Gage's side.

I know Gage wouldn't want anybody to see him like this, but I couldn't say no to him or his mom.

With as much grace as I can muster, I slide off the bed so as not to wake Gage and make my way over to Marco. I gently nudge him, causing him to wake abruptly. I quickly place my finger over my mouth, signaling for silence, and then turn my gaze back to Gage, who is still peacefully sleeping.

"There's somewhere I need to be. You need to stay with him and don't let anyone in."

"It's not safe for you to be out by yourself," Marco says.

"Don't worry about me right now. Worry about protecting your brother. He's the top priority. Call me right away if he wakes up."

I slowly retreat to the bed, gently pressing a kiss to Gage's cheek before whispering in his ear, "I'll be right back. I love you."

When I walk out of the room, Vinny is right next to Gage's mom. "Keep him safe."

Vinny nods his head while I give Gage's mom a quick hug.

As I drive to my apartment, tears stream down my face. The strange blend of numbness and despair that's been my companion for the past couple of days are suffocating me. I need to feel something besides a chaotic void, and I believe only one thing will help ground me and make me feel like myself again.

Showing everyone a strong, calm facade has been exhausting because, on the inside, I'm quaking with feelings of the unknown. But I'm determined to be what Gage needs since he became what I needed.

My eyes shift to my rearview mirror on my second-to-last left turn before I get to my condo. A spine-chilling sensation runs through me as I notice a navy-blue SUV following me extremely close. I gas it and pass my condo while watching my company keep pace behind me. Gage's gun sits uncomfortably behind my back in the waistband of my pants, but it's a welcome sensation.

"Alexa...call Vic," I say.

"Calling... Vic."

"Is he okay?" Vic murmurs into the other line with worry clear in his voice.

"He's still sleeping. I had to leave, but I think I have company."

"You left? Where are you?"

"West Adams and South Jefferson."

Vic murmurs something to someone on his end while I continue to check behind me. With glasses adorning their face and the car's visor lowered, it is difficult to identify the figure in the dimming sunlight of the afternoon.

"Julian has eyes on you through the traffic cams. Someone reported the SUV behind you stolen yesterday. You think it's the guy we're looking for?"

"Could be," I say as I make a right and punch it. My gas light pings on, and I close my eyes in resignation. Fucking great. "My gas light just came on. I need to—"

The back of my car gets rammed, and I let out a startled gasp as I grip the wheel tighter.

"What happened?"

"They hit the back of my car. I need—"

A wave of frustration washes over me, causing me to pause and shake my head. I can't continue to have someone come to my rescue every time I'm in trouble. I need to find the strength and resilience in myself to become my own hero. My own protector. I need to stand on my own two feet and prove why I'm capable of being one of the first female capos of the Chicago Mafia.

"Look, I'll give you my location if I need cleanup, but I have to go," I say as I hang up while he yells something from the other end.

Zooming through an alley behind a chain of restaurants, I decide to come to an abrupt halt next to a green metal dumpster. As the SUV screeches to a stop behind me, I yank open my door and retrieve Gage's gun, ready for whatever may come. I squint through the headlights of the SUV as I point the gun at the driver behind the wheel.

The door creaks open and Brad casually steps out as if he didn't almost run me off the road. His long-sleeved blue button-up is untucked from his wrinkled khaki pants and seems to be askew, as if he didn't line the buttons up correctly. But what makes my hand tremble is the unhinged expression in his eyes.

"Alexa. I've been waiting for you," he says as he advances on me.

"Don't come any closer," I blurt as I continue to re-aim the barrel at his head the closer he advances on me.

"Put the gun down and let's talk." He takes another step in my direction, and I don't even think as I aim the gun south, squeeze the trigger, and hit him in the outer quadrant of the left thigh.

In shock, his eyes widen, and a pained hiss escapes his lips as he limps toward me like a deranged zombie.

The slightest tremor runs through my hands as I ready myself for a chest shot, but just as I'm about to shoot, the sound of tires screeching interrupts us from behind. As he spins and retreats to his vehicle, the sound of someone pounding the pavement behind me grows louder.

"Fuck, are you okay?" Vic asks at my side.

"Yeah, follow him."

"Trey's already on it. Why don't you come with me, and I'll have one of the guys pick up your car?"

I shake my head while I continue to stare at the empty concrete where Brad was.

"The same thing still stands. Find him, then call me. I have somewhere I'm trying to go."

Without waiting for a response, I spin around and head back to my car. I place the gun on the passenger seat so I don't burn my backside, and then drive away.

Pushing open the door to my condo, I'm greeted by the sight of chaos that remains from the other day. I rush to my bedroom and start clawing through the scraps of material and anything else I can find for the little black box with the red bow. If something happened to it, it would tip me over the edge.

Tears fall freely to the ground as I sit on my hands and knees while searching everywhere for the box. My hands finally feel something under my bed, and once I grab onto it, my eyes close in relief.

Sitting on the floor, I press my back against the side of the bed, my fingers trembling as I open the box and carefully retrieve the note.

When you need direction, I will guide you, and when you need reassurance, I will comfort you. I will forever be by your side. I love you. — Your future husband, Gage

Clutching the note against my chest, I surrender to another overwhelming wave of tears, letting them escape without restraint as I sob uncontrollably. What if he doesn't make it? I can't do this without him. I can't live without him by my side. He's the love of my life. My best friend.

The sound of footsteps approaching causes my eyes to widen, and without hesitation, I draw my gun and point it at the door.

With her hands raised in surrender, Jenna materializes in the doorframe. She looks significantly healthier compared to how she appeared just two days prior.

"You can kill me if you want. I won't allow anyone else but you to do the honors."

"Do you still want all the best songs played at your funeral?" I ask.

"Only if my death is sufficient, and you take pity on me."

A small grin touches my lips, which causes her to grin as well. Despite the unresolved matters between us, my intuition tells me she has genuinely been on my side, offering her protection all these months since we've been friends.

Once I ensure the safety is on, I securely stow the gun in the back of my pants.

"I was just getting to the good part. Do you want to listen with me?" I say, holding out the iPod.

"I thought you'd never ask," she says as she walks over, does a spin, and then sits cross-legged with a grimace.

"How's the leg doing?"

"I've had worse," she says with a sad smile.

"At some point, I'm going to want to know everything."

She nods, her face sullen. "And I'll give it to you. Whatever you want to know."

"Is Jenna even your real name?"

She shakes her head. "No, but I like the name Jenna."

"What's your real name?"

"I-I don't know."

I quirk a brow. "How can you not know?"

"It's complicated." She sighs. "I... remember nothing before the age of seven."

"I don't understand."

"I was taken. All of us were. We only know what's been beaten into us."

"Jesus, Jenna."

"Let's worry about my life later. There are far more important things happening," she deflects.

"But..."

She shakes her head and I drop it. This is a lot to unpack, and she may not be ready to discuss it, as she claims. My friend, who I've grown to love like a sister over the past few months, isn't who she portrayed. Beneath the bubbly exterior of the fun-loving woman is a lost and hurting girl, and I want to help her heal and get revenge on whoever caused her pain.

I give her the earbud for her right ear while I take the left. I hit shuffle, and we wait in silence until a song plays.

The speakers come alive with the smooth, seductive notes of a song that starts slow and sensual, and in seconds, we're cracking up.

"I knew it was a playlist for your honeymoon!"

We both move back and forth as the rest of the song plays and wait for the next song. It begins with a slow tempo, and a smooth melody fills the air, triggering recognition in me. As I sob, Jenna's firm grasp on my hand offers solace throughout the entire song.

I snatch my phone from my side as it vibrates. Vic texted me an address, but it's not their house or the lake—it's somewhere else entirely.

"I have to go," I say to Jenna as I remove the left earbud and rise to my feet.

"I understand." With a frown, she nods and gives me back the other earbud.

"Do you want to come? It's somewhere in Wilding."

"I know where it is."

"Good, let's go," I say as I pocket the box with the iPod and note in it. "On the way, you can tell me all about these 'games' Trey was talking to you about the other day."

"Ugh, don't remind me."

With the night closing in, the tall trees lining the road loom large. Their branches create a dark tunnel as we drive closer to our destination. Finally, we stop just outside a massive metal gate, its imposing presence casting a shadow over us. A figure that looks vaguely familiar approaches with a gun securely fastened to his chest. With a squinted gaze, he points toward someone, signaling for them to allow us entry. We drive through the entrance and find a parking spot close to the front of the gigantic building.

"Gage is going to kill me when he finds out you came by your—" Vic says as he looks beyond me at the other side of the car where Jenna is exiting. "He's definitely going to kill me."

As I step into the vast, open area, the absence of sound is palpable, creating an eerie atmosphere that is almost unsettling. When I asked them to find him, my heart was heavy with hurt, my mind filled with confusion, and my thoughts consumed with worry about the unknown.

Rage is the only thing that pumps through my veins now.

We descend into the dimly lit basement, making our way through a narrow hallway until we reach a doorway. Brad sits on a chair inside, bound and naked, with his head drooping to the side.

I walk into the room and catch Trey and Marcus in the corner. Their laughter halts as they glance in my direction. They share a quiet demeanor, yet I discern a variance between them. As Trey's eyes meet Jenna's, his face breaks into a wide grin, his excitement evident, while Marcus purposely averts his gaze. Weird.

As I glance at her, I notice her eyes rolling with exasperation before returning her attention to the purpose of our visit.

"He's not dead, is he?" I ask, my gaze fixed on the superficial wound on his thigh—a long, shallow graze, still faintly bleeding from my earlier, clumsy shot.

"He passed out after pissing himself. We only fucked with him a little. Highly disappointing if you ask me," Trey says.

Jenna gives my hand one reassuring squeeze as I step forward and walk up to him by myself.

This is what I was trained to do, what has always been expected of me, but I was too worried I'd never have what it takes.

I guess all it takes is someone shooting the love of your life to become a vengeful, rage-infested being whose sole purpose is to destroy the person who hurt your heart and soul.

Feeling the weight of my gun against my back, I reach behind me and retrieve it. The safety clicks, the sound reverberating through the hushed room.

The gun is steady in my grip as I take aim at his left foot, and the tension in the air intensifies as I squeeze the trigger.

At that moment, I don't know what's more satisfying—the piercing sound of his scream or the sight of crimson blood staining the concrete floor.

His tear-filled eyes bore into mine, radiating a hatred that I undeniably reflect.

"When did you first start following me?"

"I'm not telling you shit," Brad says as he howls in pain.

As I position the muzzle of the gun on top of his kneecap, he struggles, but the tight bindings keep him from making any significant movement.

"Answer the question."

"High school!"

The mere idea of someone stalking me for all these years sends shivers down my spine and fills me with dread because I never noticed.

"You're part of the gang?"

When he doesn't answer, I aim the gun at his knee as he clenches his lips, and with a single shot, I shatter his kneecap. The sound of another piercing scream fills the air, causing him to convulse and vomit on the unforgiving concrete room.

"Answer my questions or I'll just keep riddling you with gunshot wounds."

"No. My brother—" he says as he cries. "He let me go with him to watch you, but then he said I couldn't come that night because I found out they were going to kill you, but I wanted you. I watched you. I saw you first. You were mine."

I ignore his delusions and continue with my interrogation. "Are you the one who left me roses and fucked up my condo?"

"We were supposed to be together, not you and that guy... I hope he's dead."

The intense rage that's been simmering for the past few days suddenly erupts. With a forceful motion, I press the gun against his other knee, noting the hard metal against my palm before pulling the trigger for the third time.

An unprecedented surge of adrenaline courses through me, making my hands tremble violently. I let out a deep breath with a need to finish this. Bending toward him, I whisper, "There is only one person I will ever love, and it'll never be you."

With a steady hand, I press the gun firmly against his heart before finally squeezing the trigger. Once he slumps over, I turn around and face Jenna, Vic, Trey, Marcus, and Julian.

No disapproval, hatred, or disgust is reflected in their eyes, only acceptance and pride. It's a fucked-up thing after what I just did, but that is my life. That is the Mafia. And when someone comes after your family, your loved one, you eliminate them. No remorse, no second thoughts.

I finish putting the safety back on and tuck it into the back of my jeans just as Jenna walks up to me.

She takes my hand, and her mouth goes to my ear. "You found your power. Your strength. I always knew you had it in you, and now you do too."

The power and strength she speaks of, a fiery current now coursing through my veins, is fueled by a love so immense, so incandescent, it transcends the boundaries of life and death.

I now fully understand why Dad can do it effortlessly, without even flinching. His essence is preserved by the boundless love he holds for us, and reciprocally, the love we hold for him.

"I want to go back and be with Gage," I say to Jenna. I turn back to the guys just as I hit the doorframe. "Thank you for finding him so quickly, and thank you for this."

Thirty

Gage

My eyes open slightly as I hear a beep accompanied by a searing pain in my abdomen. A dim light hangs above my uncomfortable bed, and the smell of antiseptic makes me nauseous.

I attempt to move, but my right arm feels weighed down. I gaze that way and notice a full head of shiny dark hair I'd recognize anywhere. My lips pull into a smirk as I take my right hand, which sports an IV tube running through the back of it, and touch her soft hair. The movement makes me wince as I feel a pinch in my abdomen, but I still seize the opportunity to smell her.

Why am I here, and why is my stomach so fucking sore?

I push the thin white sheet and blanket that sits mid-chest down, then pull up the white and blue hospital gown. A large incision runs down the right side of my abdomen. It fucked up the skull tattoo Vic inked onto my body.

Memories swirl in my mind, creating a disorganized puzzle as I attempt to piece together how I ended up in this situation.

We had a meeting, found out Marco had valid reasons for his actions when we were younger, no matter how fucked up they were. Alexa and I went to Rosie and Vic's. She's fucking pregnant. I still can't believe that asshole got her pregnant before they got married. Jenna's the fucking assassin. I always felt something was off about her. My mind then moves on to every glorious detail of Alexa and me in the club. Thank fuck for remembering that.

I close my eyes for a minute, and then it all hits. That stupid motherfucker shot me while declaring his love for my girl, and then pain. So much fucking pain.

I grab onto the metal bed rail and try to pull myself up, but I just fall back into the pillows with a thud. The exertion has me huffing and panting in pain. I despise being weak, and now I have someone who needs to die immediately. This won't do.

"Easy, baby bro. It's the first time you've been awake in almost a week. Take it easy."

I turn my gaze to see Marco sitting in a chair in the room's corner. His hair sticks out in all different directions, and dark circles surround his eyes.

"You look like shit," I rasp.

"Not as bad as you," he says as he rises from his chair and hands me a cup with a straw. "Here."

"Where the fuck is he, and why wasn't I woken up sooner?"

"He's dead, and you had complications on your way here and in surgery. Your body needed time to heal."

"You know I would've wanted to end him myself."

"It wasn't my call," Marco says with a shrug.

"Whose was it, then?"

He nods his head over to Alexa, who's still lightly snoring on my side.

"She made the call?"

Marco nods. "And carried out the execution."

My eyes widen as I glance back at my girl. The thought of her taking care of him fills me with pride.

"They said the second you wake up to let them know; I'll be back."

"Thank you," I murmur, hoping this will be the beginning of a mend between us.

Alexa startles from the click of the door closing and her big blue eyes gaze up at me. "You're awake!"

"Or dreaming," I say as I caress her cheek. "If I knew all it took was a hospital stay to get you laying by my side, I would've gotten hurt sooner."

"Don't you dare make jokes. I almost lost you," she says with a hitch in her voice as she wipes the sleeve of her gray sweatshirt across her glassy eyes.

"Even in death, I'll never leave you, Lex," I say as I grab her face and pull her toward me. "I love you."

"I love you too, Gage," she says as her lips meet mine.

Epilogue

"**H**urry up!" Alexa yells at me from the top of the flower-covered hill.

"I'm moving. It's not like I almost died a month ago or anything," I grumble as I hold my still sore stomach.

"I got shot, too, and you don't see me complaining," she says, lifting her short sleeve to reveal the barely healed wound on her right arm where the bullet grazed her one week ago as we were leaving the grocery store. The fucking grocery store. The assassin group is relentless, and although they're dropping like flies, it's like a zombie attack. As we kill them, they multiply.

Just as I get to the top of the hill, Alexa extends her arm, and I see the pear-shaped solitaire I put on her finger two weeks ago glisten in the sunset. I feel for mine on my left hand with my thumb and smirk. The weight of the ring feels good on my finger, especially knowing Alexa placed it there.

I glance across the field covered in reds, oranges, whites, and pinks, with the magnificent sunset in the background, and then gaze back at Alexa. Should we be on a honeymoon right now while everything is imploding? Probably not, but I got a wake up call after almost dying. Your next breath isn't guaranteed and Alexa's expression of awe as she stands beside me makes it all worth it. She is worth it. Always has been, always will be.

When we return, the fight will still be waiting for us, and I'll relish every moment of dismantling our enemies with Alexa at my side.

"I love this," Alexa says as she glances over at me.

"And I love you," I say as I pull her closer to me and devour the sweet skin right under her ear.

"Gage," she says with a surprised smile as she pulls away, which has been her usual since she figured out she loves me just as much as I love her. "Someone might come."

"Let them," I say as I pull her down onto my lap so she is facing me and her legs wrap around my waist.

I unfasten my leather belt and work down my zipper. Alexa looks around the landscape before her eyes find mine again.

"We can't," she says.

Gently, I trail my hand up her toned leg, savoring the sensation of her smooth skin underneath my touch. "There was a reason you wore a skirt like this, Lex," I say as I finger the brown-and-tan plaid skirt, which will be in my dreams way after we leave our honeymoon. So much so that I'm considering adding a teacher-student room to the club because of this.

My fingers glide under her skirt and all that greets me are her silky wet folds. I let out a groan. "Did my good girl do this for me, too, huh?"

Alexa's face heats as her teeth grab her pouty, red bottom lip. "I may have taken them off at the restaurant earlier."

"Ah, so you were a bad girl and have been walking around like this for hours?" I smirk while I continue wreaking havoc on her clit, which elicits a chorus of moans. "Whatever should I do with you?"

I glance around the field once more, but it's relatively deserted, besides a few people milling around quite far away. If I can only see their silhouettes, I'm sure that's all they can see on their end as well. I pull my hand out of her skirt just as her walls clench around my fingers, much to her dismay. There's only one way she'll be coming right now, and that's with me inside her.

My cock is in my hand before I give it much more thought. I crave her presence, yearn for her touch, and am utterly lost without her tight embrace around me.

"Ride me, Lex."

"You are absolutely crazy," she says with a satisfied sigh as she slowly lowers herself until we're pelvis to pelvis and our foreheads are touching.

A groan escapes my lips as I grip the back of her neck and thrust upward.

"Only for you. Forever for you."

THE END

THANK YOU

Thank you so much for reading ALL YOUR LIES! If you liked it, please leave a review. Your support means the world to me.

I also want to thank my daughter for listening to me blabber about my book ideas on our nightly walks.